1·2·3·4,
I DECLARE A THUMB WAR

GRAVEYARD GIRLS

1·2·3·4, I DECLARE A THUMB WAR

New York Times best-selling authors

LISI HARRISON · DANIEL KRAUS

Illustrated by
Flavia Sorrentino

union
square
kids

NEW YORK

**union
square
kids**

NEW YORK

UNION SQUARE KIDS and the distinctive Union Square Kids logo
are trademarks of Union Square & Co., LLC.

Union Square & Co., LLC, is a subsidiary of Sterling Publishing Co., Inc.

Text © 2022 Lisi Harrison and Daniel Kraus
Illustrations © 2022 Union Square & Co., LLC

ISBN 978-1-4549-4454-6 (hardcover)
ISBN 978-1-4549-4455-3 (e-book)

Library of Congress Cataloging-in-Publication Data

Names: Harrison, Lisi, author. | Kraus, Daniel, author.
Title: 1-2-3-4, I declare a thumb war / Lisi Harrison, Daniel Kraus.
Other titles: One, two, three, four, I declare a thumb war
Description: New York : Union Square Kids, [2022] | Series: Graveyard Girls
  | Audience: Ages 8 to 12. | Audience: Grades 4-6. | Summary: As the
  100th anniversary of the electrocution of the town's most infamous killer
  approaches, an anonymous text message lures five twelve-year-olds to the
  cemetery, inspiring the first meeting of the Graveyard Girls and setting the
  stage for a terrifying tale from Whisper that they will never forget.
Identifiers: LCCN 2022009626 (print) | LCCN 2022009627 (ebook) | ISBN
  9781454944546 (hardcover) | ISBN 9781454944553 (e-book)
Subjects: CYAC: Storytelling--Fiction. | Horror stories--Fiction. |
  Friendship--Fiction. | Middle schools--Fiction. | Schools--Fiction. |
  BISAC: JUVENILE FICTION / Horror | JUVENILE FICTION / Girls & Women |
  LCGFT: Novels.
Classification: LCC PZ7.H2527 Aah 2022 (print) | LCC PZ7.H2527 (ebook) |
  DDC [Fic]--dc23
LC record available at https://lccn.loc.gov/2022009626
LC ebook record available at https://lccn.loc.gov/2022009627

For information about custom editions, special sales, and
premium purchases, please contact specialsales@unionsquareandco.com.

Printed in the United States of America

Lot #:

2 4 6 8 10 9 7 5 3 1

07/22

unionsquareandco.com

Cover and interior illustrations by Flavia Sorrentino
Texture on printed case is vldkont/Shutterstock.com
Cover design by Jo Obarowski
Interior design by Christine Heun

To all future final girls.
You've got this.

CHAPTER 1

SILAS HOKE

I've had my eye on these girls for a while now.

Sixth graders. Best friends. Consumed with their dramatic little lives.

I know their names: Whisper, Frannie, Sophie, and Gemma. I know who their families are. I know where they live. How did I learn all this?

How do you think?

Killers come in all shapes and sizes, but most have one skill in common.

The ability to creep up on you.

And I've been creeping.

The most delicious part is that these girls live in Misery Falls, Oregon.

The same place I lived.

The same place I died.

I know this town. Its corners. Its alleys. Its hiding spots. Most of all, its dead ends.

And Misery Falls is one giant dead end. Escape is impossible.

My miserable life was proof of that. So was my miserable death.

Once a month, these four girls get together for a good old-fashioned, up-all-night sleepover, during which one tells the others a "scary" story. They call themselves the Grim Sleepers.

Cute, right?

Wrong.

Their stories aren't grim. And I won't stand for cutesy substitutes that give a bad name to fear—the purest, most delicious emotion in the world.

They say they want to be scared, but do they really?

Can Whisper the track star outrun fear?

Will Frannie the actress perform bravely?

Is Straight A Sophie clever enough to outsmart *me*?

And then there's Gemma, their leader. The only one who really believes in the supernatural. Smart girl—but

her so-called spirit guides are going to scatter when they sense my presence.

I'm going to give the Grim Sleepers something *real* to be afraid of.

Soon.

Very, very soon.

CHAPTER 2

WHISPER

It was all about atmos*fear*.

If Whisper Martin could make her bedroom darker than a closed casket and play an eerie song full of ghastly moans, the girls of the Grim Sleepers just might—a big *might*—forgive her last disaster.

✳

A month ago, it had been Whisper's turn to host the sleepover, meaning it was her turn to tell a story so scary that Sophie, Frannie, and Gemma would beg to keep a light on at bedtime and fall asleep holding hands. There was just one problem: scary stories were, well, *scary*, and Whisper's life was already scary enough.

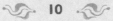

That's why she'd named her story "The Sensitive Spirit." It had zero to do with evil beings, bloodthirsty revenge, or ominous footsteps and everything to do with a twelve-year-old dead girl who took offense to the expression "pale as a ghost." Think: cautionary tale about the effects of negative body image.

Everyone said they appreciated the message. But that was all they appreciated.

"Maybe the sensitive spirit could *do* something," Sophie had said, "instead of walking around being sensitive the whole time."

Sophie Wexler was the picture of success, just like everyone else in the Wexler family. In class, Sophie liked to lean forward, ready to raise her hand first— always with the right answer. She used a mix of colorful hair bands to pull her flat-ironed curls away from her studious face. A face that had settled into its usual *I'm not judging, I'm helping* look.

"What do you mean, 'do something'?" Whisper had blurted.

Blurt was what Whisper did. Her tiny frame, thick glasses, pale skin, and beanies—always beanies, even in summer—made her look meek, and she was often overlooked. So, at a young age, she learned to speak up. Way up. After years of being told to whisper, Willow Martin became known as Whisper Martin. Her name changed, but her vocal volume did not.

"I dunno," Sophie had said. "Maybe something a little more . . . *creepy?*"

"But the sensitive spirit shared her secrets with a one-eyed cat. Isn't *that* creepy?" Whisper blurted, again.

"I've got four words for you," Frannie said. "*More drama* and *less trauma.*"

Frannie Vargas-Stein had a springy explosion of brown curls that bounced when she moved her arms. Which was *alllll* the time. *That's what actors do,* Frannie often said. *We communicate with our entire body.* Frannie's attitude was also a springy explosion. She'd wear anything and outperform anyone. The more people watching, the better.

"*More drama and less trauma* is five words," Sophie had pointed out.

"It's four. *And* is not a real word," Frannie insisted.

"Since when?" Sophie asked.

"Since Pluto stopped being a planet." Frannie flashed her stage-light smile. "I swear. Google it."

"Google *this!*" Sophie chucked one of her precious pieces of candy corn at Frannie. It landed with a *donk* in the middle of Frannie's forehead. Everyone cracked up except Whisper, who groaned.

"Tina wants to send out a joint holiday card. Her family *and* my family. Together," Whisper said. "It's going to say *Season's Greetings from the Martins And the Pollards*. And the *and* was definitely capitalized."

Tina.

Talk about scary. Whisper's dad's girlfriend had moved into the house nine months ago and was rapidly taking over every room. Sure, it had been five years since Jenny, Whisper's mom and a beloved pastry chef, died. But did Tina really have to block Jenny's pictures with her own? Whisper had begged her father to kick Tina out (three times!). But Miles, Whisper's ten-year-old brother, was so excited to have a full-time playmate in Tina's son, Rayne, that *he* begged to let them stay.

Of course, Miles won.

Worst of all, Tina had a daughter who also happened to be the scariest popular girl in Whisper's class—a well-styled, vanilla-scented monster named Paisley Pollard. Yes, *that* Paisley Pollard. The one who drop-kicked Whisper's Furby into a pile of fresh doggie doo back in first grade.

"Back to Whisper's story," Gemma had said. "I give it a two."

Gemma had the sturdiness of a girl who grew up milking cows on a dairy farm—not restocking tarot cards at

the Spirit Sanctuary, the metaphysical supply shop owned by Gemma's mother and aunt. Golden skin, butter-blonde waves of hair, and the kind of eyes so icy blue, they might possibly see into other worlds. Which is exactly what Gemma tried to do. Spirits, ghosts, cryptids, reincarnation, ESP—you name it, Gemma believed it. And she was determined to make her best friends believe it, too.

"A two?!" Whisper had giggle-shouted. "It wasn't *that* bad, was it?"

Gemma was the creator of the Scream Scale, a one-to-ten rating system they used to rate Grim Sleepers stories. She had never rated anyone higher than a seven. But a two?

"That's—that's—that's lower than Frannie's story about the zombie cheerleaders!" Whisper had cried.

"'The Zom-Pom Girls.' Not my best effort," Frannie admitted.

"It's lower than Sophie's werewolf who couldn't stop laughing!"

"'The story about the Were-LOLf,'" Sophie recalled ruefully. "I wrote it on the bus ride back from Model UN. It had been a long day solving global crises."

The good news was that Whisper's friends had voted to allow her the first do-over in Grim Sleepers history, and Whisper had gratefully accepted.

⁕

Fast-forward to now, one month later: Whisper was ready to roll. Her room was set and her look complete. Black eye shadow. Black fingernails. Black lipstick. And the coup de grâce—the official Grim Sleepers cloak.

Okay, it was a nubby hooded bathrobe, previously yellow but now dyed black. Gemma once said their cloaks looked "sad," but Whisper, a nature-loving environmentalist, preferred "sustainable."

Whisper checked her phone: 6:12 p.m. All gatherings started at exactly thirteen minutes past the hour. One time Gemma heard her mother call the number thirteen "the devil's dozen" and thought it was super goose pimply. They all did.

Lights off, Whisper sat on her bed and waited for their signal. This was the spookiest part. Spindly branches tapped her window, each twig skeleton-gray in the moonlight.

Then a drop of blood hit the window glass. Whisper gasped, and her skin prickled. She knew it was the red light from Gemma's laser pointer, but it jump-scared her every time.

Whisper lifted the hood of her cloak and hurried for the door, feet bare so Paisley and her friends wouldn't hear her pass. They'd taken over the living room, same as every Saturday night when Dad and Tina went out. It smelled like nail polish, Paisley's vanilla shampoo, and attitude. But their *sounds* bothered Whisper the most. *Click, clack, tick, tap*—their thumbnails beat against the keypads of their phones as they typed, liked, texted, and posted. It made Whisper think of cockroaches scuttling across a tin roof.

Chilly autumn air rushed inside when Whisper opened the front door to find three girls staring back at her. Dull eyes. No smiles. Hoods low. Still as cadavers. Dead leaves swirling around their black high-top sneakers. Even though they had done this dozens of times before, Whisper still thought her friends looked scary.

She wiggled her fingers, silently summoning them to follow her upstairs. Because of Gemma's strict no-talking-until-we-reach-the-bedchamber rule, Whisper added a head tilt, to warn them of Paisley and the ClikTok Squad. But when they tried to sneak past the living room, Whisper heard the unmistakable *ka-sss* of a phone camera.

"Look! It's a poop parade!"

Paisley Pollard. Twelve going on insufferable. Wearing her mother's lavender silk pajamas and maroon Dr. Martens. Laughing, displaying the space between her front teeth that sixth-grade boys mysteriously thought was hot.

"Uh, nice costumes, but Hoke Week doesn't start until Monday, freaks."

Miranda Young.

Whisper imagined Frannie's curls tightening like coiled snakes.

Frannie and Miranda had been best friends and theater buddies until fourth grade. Then, thanks to "the incident," they became best enemies. Whisper had asked Frannie for details a billion times, but Frannie never talked about it. "I'll tell you someday," she'd say in that breathless way of hers. Like some weary old Hollywood actress who had seen a thing or two but was too tired to dish.

Not that Whisper blamed Frannie for taking issue with Miranda. For one thing, the girl wore yellow-tinted sunglasses. Indoors. At night. She said the tinted lenses blocked harmful blue light from her phone, thereby saving her precious violet-blue eyes from becoming basic brown—you know, like Frannie's.

"I can't believe we have a whole week of events for some dead psycho," Paisley muttered, then returned to her phone. "This town is tragic. And you four are *extra* trag—"

"I like Hoke Week."

The comment came from the third girl in the living room, Zuzu Otsuka. Japanese American. Sleek

shoulder-length hair with a bold purple streak, the kind that skims eyelashes and hides secrets. She was rocking camouflage drop-crotch pants, an intentionally ripped cashmere sweater, and reflective gold sneakers. No surprise there. Her parents owned Jōhin—a boutique clothing and accessories brand based in Misery Falls and worn by all the most influential influencers.

Zuzu wasn't just the Otsukas' daughter. She was their social media muse.

And just like she did in so many marketing posts, Zuzu was popping her trademark cinnamon gum. Whisper was certain she could smell it from across the room.

Pop!

"I guess Hoke Week *is* kind of nostalgic," Paisley allowed.

"I bet the Turd Herd will be there," Miranda said loudly enough for the Grim Sleepers to hear.

Paisley snorted. "Turd Herd. Ohmigod. I'm so posting that."

"Not if I post it first!" Miranda laughed.

Click, clack, tick, tap.

Whisper wanted to shout, *I hope your thumbs fall off!* Shouting, after all, was what she did best. But Gemma's vow of silence was an ironclad rule.

Whisper did have another talent. Two months into sixth grade and she was already one of the top runners on Misery Falls Middle School's track team, with Coach Redmond choosing her to anchor every relay race. So, she'd use that talent now and run away from these keypad-melting villains before she blurted something she'd regret.

Cheeks scorching and heart revving, Whisper lowered her head and raced upstairs. The clatter of texting and the popping of Zuzu's gum chased her the whole way.

CHAPTER 3

WHISPER

"You see how it is? Living with her?" Whisper exploded once they were safely in her bedroom. Crypt black as it was, the girls knew their way around and gathered on her not-so-scary daisy-print bedspread. "I swear! If my dad marries Tina, I'm going to—"

"*Shhhhh!*" the other three girls hissed.

"Your dad has had girlfriends before," Frannie said softly. "It won't last."

"But they never moved in. Like bedbugs," Whisper said as angry, frustrated feelings marched up from her belly and into her mouth. "Tina's first husband dumped her, you know. He moved to a whole other state, and I don't blame him."

"You're not moving to another state," Sophie said. "Your dad will wise up. You'll see."

"And if he doesn't . . . ?"

Frannie shrugged. "Maybe you just need to get to know her better."

Whisper sighed. Her mom's death had taught her a lot about time and what it can and can't do for pain. Grief was like Whisper herself: unable to stay quiet. It was forever shouting. Desperate to be heard—and afraid of being forgotten.

"I'm so over the whole mean girl thing." Sophie sighed. "It *is* scientifically possible for the ClikTok Squad to be popular *and* nice."

"And 'Turd Herd'? Really? Our cloaks are black, not brown," Gemma said. "Anyway, 'Poop Troupe' would have been funnier."

The sound of a pillow making contact with Gemma's face followed. Then giggles.

"I don't know about Miranda's number twos, but my poops don't wear glasses," Whisper said.

"TMI!" Frannie announced.

"Since when is anything between us TMI?" Sophie asked.

"TMI: Totally My Intestines," Frannie said. "I was agreeing. My poops don't wear glasses, either. Just earrings."

They laughed even harder, so hard that Whisper fell off the bed. It knocked the air out of her, and she coughed until she had tears in her eyes. Her friends always knew how to make her feel better.

Then—*zzzzzip.*

Gemma was opening her duffel bag.

Without another word, the Grim Sleepers moved to the floor and sat in a circle. Knee to knee, hoods up. Talking was once again forbidden.

A white flame burst upward, then fattened into a pumpkin orange. Gemma had struck the ceremonial match.

It was time.

Her eyes flashed as she touched the flame to a gold candle. The wick took the fire with a *snap*, and a demonic glow spread across the girls' faces. The back of Whisper's neck prickled. Two years after the club began, the invocation still delivered a tingly thrill.

"I, Gemma Garrett, call to order this gathering of the Grim Sleepers."

She held out the bejeweled Chalice of Cherubs— one of many items sold at the Spirit Sanctuary. Exactly how a nonbiodegradable cup destined to leak toxins into the soil for the next four hundred and fifty years was spiritual, Whisper didn't know. The store seemed to use the term very loosely, applying it to crystals, smudge sticks, chakra pendants, dream catchers, Tibetan sound bowls, and everything else it sold. But Whisper tried to let that go on the off chance that Gemma's spirit guides and guardian angels were real. In which case, they were probably looking out for the planet, too.

Whisper took the Chalice of Cherubs. As host, it was her job to fill it with "blood." She poured the cranberry juice, took a sip, and passed it to her left.

After everyone drank, Whisper lit the incense, started her spooky playlist, and then gave the nod. The chanting began:

"Come, ghost,
Come, monster,
Come, devilkin,
Tonight's story is about to begin."

Three times they repeated it, and with every round, Whisper felt the usual cold quake of fear. Yet she took comfort in the fact that *she* was the one telling the story. *She* was in control. She lifted the candle to her face and basked in its flickering warmth.

The others leaned in.

"Toniiiiiight," she began, drawing out the word long enough to earn an extra point on the Scream Scale, "I will teeeeeell you the taaaaaale of the—"

Thud. Thud.

Whisper lowered the candle. "Did you hear that?"

"Hear what?" Sophie asked.

"Footsteps."

"Is this part of the performance?" Frannie asked.

Gemma beamed. "I like it. Way to step it up."

It wasn't part of anything. But the last thing she wanted to do was get scared in front of her friends before she'd even started her story. She listened again, heard nothing, and decided to continue.

"Silence!" Whisper hissed. "Toniiiiiight, I will tell the eerie anecdote of—"

Sophie giggled. "'Eerie anecdote'?"

Gemma cleared her throat—a warning to heed decorum.

"Of the vaccinated vampire," Whisper finished.

Frannie's laugh sputtered out between pressed lips.

"Frannie!" Gemma chided.

"I'm sorry! But how can he be scary if he's all, like, health conscious?"

"He was wearing a caaaape, that's howwww," Whisper continued, "and his name was Vincent."

Frannie giggled again. "Vincent the Vampire?"

"Yessssss," Whisper said. "And on this night, Vincent was walking through town, moaning and clutching his arm—"

"Why?" Gemma sounded excited. "What happened to his arm?"

"It hurt . . ."—Whisper let the pause stretch out, milking it for maximum terror—". . . from the vacciiiiine."

CHAPTER 4

SOPHIE

Sophie didn't sit down at her usual lunch table. She collided with it. Her glass of sparkling water sloshed past the rim, spilling all over her veggie burger. Not that it mattered—lunch period was practically over anyway. It was Monday, and only the second week of sixth grade, and already she was too busy with extra-curriculars to eat.

"What did I miss?" she asked as she settled in beside Frannie.

"Gemma was just about to tell us what Vincent the Vampire said when he got turned away from the blood bank."

Sophie took a napkin from Whisper's tray and attempted to dry her burger. "What did he say?"

"'It was worth a *shot!*'" Gemma said.

Everyone laughed except Whisper, who sighed. "Such a dad joke. Well, back when my dad still told jokes."

Gemma, pretending to be offended, tossed a french fry at Whisper, who caught it in midair, dipped it in Frannie's milkshake, and folded it into her mouth.

Sophie wilted a little. Gemma was such a standout in her flowy bohemian dresses and take-charge attitude. Frannie was larger than life and fun. Whisper cared more about the planet than the way she looked, and she could run faster than most eighth graders.

But Sophie? Look at her—she was a stress-case perfectionist who was *drying a wet bun.* She wanted to be confident like Gemma, fun-loving like Frannie, and passionate like Whisper, but Sophie was too busy to be anything other than, well, busy. Busy and worried.

Joking aside, Whisper's tale of Vincent the Vampire had been so tame that Sophie worried it might mark the beginning of the end for the Grim Sleepers. And that scared her more than anything.

Their monthly sleepovers were the only study-free, practice-free, pressure-free "me time" that Sophie had. Where else could she write a terrible story just to

experience the thrill of failure? Sure, she'd acted disappointed when Gemma gave "The Were-LOLf" a three on the Scream Scale. But in truth? Sophie had been elated. Failing felt exhilarating. It made her heart pound so hard she could feel it all the way to her scalp. Colors appeared brighter, sounds sharper. It was risky. It was deceptive. It was wrong. And yet she had never felt more alive.

Frannie nudged her. "Where were you, anyway?"

"Huh?"

"Why were you late for lunch?"

"Let me guess," Gemma said. "You were signing up for a new math class and for every single position on student council."

Sophie folded her bun-drying napkin with her usual tidiness. "First, there's no such thing as *new* math. Second, you don't sign up for student council, you get elected. And third, no one can run for every position."

The other three girls exchanged quick glances, then shouted, "Relax Attack!"

Suddenly they were leaning over their trays, playfully pinching Sophie.

It was their way of letting Sophie know that she was taking herself too seriously—or her friends too literally. Sometimes Relax Attacks happened multiple times per day.

"We know how elections work!" Frannie pinched.

"And that there's no such thing as new math!" Whisper poked.

"What would that even be?" Gemma tickled. "Algebrometry? Geomulus? Calcubra?"

"Count Calcubra!" Sophie managed while swatting them away.

"Vincent the Vampire's cousin!" Frannie cried.

They all cracked up, but no one laughed harder than Sophie. She needed this release after a day full of fanatical note taking and overparticipation—all while maintaining perfect posture, by the way. Her lifelong mission of trying to be as good as, if not better than, her older sister, Jade, was exhausting.

Mostly because she had yet to pull it off.

The issue wasn't her parents. Meg and Clarence Wexler encouraged Sophie to slow down, cut her workload, and smell the flowers—a pastime that would only exacerbate her allergies. To Sophie, it sounded like her parents didn't believe she had Jade potential. So, she needed to keep pushing until they thought she could handle everything that Jade could.

"If you must know, I was signing up to help Ms. Silver decorate the school's float for Friday's Hoke Folk parade. Which reminds me . . ."

"That's right!" Gemma smacked her hands on the table. "Today's the first day of Hoke Week. Which means one of us must tell the tale. Whose turn is it this year? Sophie?"

Sophie nodded. It was indeed her turn. She checked her phone. Six minutes until the bell rings. Six minutes to tell a ten-minute story. *Challenge accepted!*

She cast a mysterious glance around the table. This was hardly a Grim Sleepers gathering—daylight, crowded cafeteria, street clothes, soggy-bun smells—but Sophie was determined to crush it anyway. She always did.

"Back in the early days of Misery Falls," she began, "there was a boarding school called Saint Bernadette's School for Girls. They had a PE instructor named Silas Hoke. He was a typical gym teacher in some ways—loud, mean, demanding. But he was also different. For one, Silas Hoke had a wooden left leg."

Whisper, Frannie, and Gemma stopped eating. The story never failed. How could it? Unlike their Grim Sleepers tales, this was true.

"Rumor has it," Sophie continued, "that Hoke was a marine in World War I. The Germans sank his ship, but he survived on a life raft with a few sailors. They were starving. One night, they drew lots to see whose limb they'd cut off to eat. Hoke drew the shortest stick. The soldiers sawed off his leg, ate it—and twenty minutes later, a boat showed up and rescued them."

Frannie made a barfy face.

"Back then, kids were really cruel to people who looked different. And the girls of Saint Bernadette's were the cruelest of all. Especially a girl named Ginny Baker, who mocked Silas Hoke. Everywhere she went she imitated the *thonk-thonk* sound of his wooden leg. Hoke's time on the life raft had given him a fear of water—and Ginny Baker used to quote-unquote *accidentally* spray him with water any time she could. All the girls laughed. But Silas Hoke? The pranks slowly drove him mad. Finally, one sleepy morning the girls at Saint Bernadette's woke up to find—"

"This is my favorite part," Gemma said excitedly.

"—Ginny Baker still in bed. Covered in blood. Dead. And that's not all. Her left leg was gone."

"We should stop there," Whisper pleaded. "The bell is about to ring."

Sophie, of course, kept going. "A single trail of blood and one bloody footprint—a right foot—led all the way to Crimson Creek Cemetery, where Hoke was using a hammer and nails . . . to attach Ginny Baker's sawed-off leg to his own."

"Ew." Frannie frowned at her tray. "Why did I get the chili corn dog?"

"In those days, Ashgate Prison was still in operation, and they had an electric chair—Old Sparky, they called it.

Once Hoke was convicted, Warden Cartwright strapped Hoke in and fired it up. But for some reason, Old Sparky had problems, and it took all night to electrocute Hoke. Between high-voltage jolts, Hoke swore he'd return to get revenge on the girls of Misery Falls.

"Legend has it that every year, on the anniversary of his death, one girl sees a flash of lightning—just like Old Sparky—and hears the *thonk-thonk* of Hoke's wooden leg getting closer. Then—*poof!* She's never heard from again. And that's why we have Hoke Week."

"Bravo!" Frannie clapped.

"Five whole days of creepy activities to celebrate a murderer," Whisper said. "I don't get it."

"We're not celebrating him, we're banishing his evil spirit from Misery Falls so he doesn't attack anyone," Gemma explained. "And it brings tons of tourists here, which is great for business at the Spirit Sanctuary. The rest of the year? It's a ghost town in there."

"If Ginny Baker had run track, Silas Hoke never would have caught her," Whisper said.

"Whatever helps you sleep at night," Gemma teased.

"That's not funny!"

The cafeteria bell rang, and a collective groan rose from the students. Lunch was over.

While the girls cleared their trays, Sophie wondered if Jade had ever told the Silas Hoke story. And if she had, who'd told it better? Her stomach dipped just thinking about it. Even her insides knew the answer.

"You guys should come by the store tonight. We can scare the tourists," Gemma said.

"I've got Photography Club," Sophie said.

"What about after that?"

"Peer tutoring."

"What about tomorrow?"

"Piano."

"Tomorrow after piano?"

"Dinner."

"After dinner?"

"Spanish vocabulary."

By this point, the girls had got rid of their trays— perfect timing for Gemma to shout, "Relax Attack!"

After the good-natured onslaught was over, Sophie hurried to Advanced English, arms swinging and heart full. Her friends, their club—they were her favorite escape. They were also her *only* escape. Yet Sophie didn't know how to be anyone but Straight A Sophie around them. Not because they wanted her to be. If anything, they encouraged her to relax, same as her parents. But their roles had been established years

ago, and Sophie was cast as the tightly wound overachiever. She couldn't let loose even if she wanted to. What would the Grim Sleepers think of a chill, average version of Sophie? Would they embrace the change or feel weirded out by it?

Sophie took her usual seat at the front of the class, opened her tidy notebook, and sat tall. Just like she always did.

Ding!

She checked her texts and found a message from a BLOCKED NUMBER. Sophie hid her phone under her desk and tapped the screen.

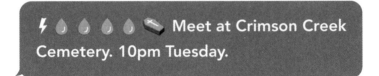

Sophie frowned. Ten o'clock? On a school night? Only Gemma would suggest something so bold. But Gemma *never* sent texts about the club. She preferred weird notes written on tree bark or inked onto burnt scraps of parchment.

But if not Gemma, then who?

Straight A Sophie was about to erase it when Chill Sophie stopped her.

Maybe we should check it out, Chill Sophie said.

And for the first time in her life, Straight A Sophie agreed.

CHAPTER 5

FRANNIE

Wind bit Frannie's cheeks as she and Whisper biked toward the town square for the kickoff of Hoke Week. The evening sky—a tie-dyed swirl of orange and navy—reminded her of the official colors of Misery Falls Middle School. *Ugh, school. Ugh, Miranda. Ugh, the school play. Ugh, Miranda and the school play!* Frannie removed one hand from the handlebars and slipped it into the warm pocket of her fleece jacket. If only she could stuff her icy heart in there, too.

"You're worrying too much!" Whisper said as they stopped at a red light on Industry Avenue. "And crying about it isn't going to help. If it did, Tina, Paisley, and Rayne would have been out of my house months ago. Washed down the sewer on a tide of my tears."

"I'm not crying, I'm sniffling," Frannie said. "And I just *can't* with another Miranda competition right now. She literally told Ms. Snowden, to her face, that she was auditioning for the lead in *Little Shop of Horrors.* Whisper—it's so unheard of that no one's ever heard of it before. Who tells a director how to cast her show?"

"I thought everyone did that."

"Maybe, but it's tacky. Anyway, I totally called her on it, and guess what she said?" The light turned green, but Frannie didn't pedal. She wanted Whisper to see the horror on her face when she delivered the news. "She said, '*Francine*, just because you have the same annoying high-pitched voice as Audrey doesn't mean you're good enough to play Audrey.'"

Frannie took off, leaving Whisper behind to absorb the audacity—a cyclist's version of the mic drop.

"She did *not* use Francine," Whisper called. "What did you say back?"

"Nothing! I was so shocked, my vocal cords seized, which is exactly what you *don't* want before an audition."

On the cold wind came the sharp spice of warm churros. Frannie couldn't help but smile a bit. Growing up in Misery Falls, and being a sucker for theatrics, she knew the Hoke Week schedule by heart.

- Monday: the Hoke Stoke—a giant bonfire in the town square to ward off Hoke's spirit
- Tuesday: the Hoke Poke—a charity blood drive in honor of Ginny Baker
- Wednesday: the Hoke Soak—a town-wide splash in ice-cold Misery Falls itself to show Hoke how *they* aren't afraid of water
- Thursday: the Hoke Smoke—a big barbecue bash to let Hoke know the locals are a united front
- Friday: the Hoke Folk—a raucous parade in front of Ashgate Prison to cleanse Misery Falls of Hoke's spirit for another year

If only Frannie could cleanse Misery Falls Middle School of Miranda.

She turned onto Steel Road, riding past the strobing brake lights of cars hunting for parking spaces. She could smell the burning logs and feel the buzz of the building crowd.

"Then, right when I thought it couldn't get any worse," she continued, "Miranda auditions with 'Somewhere That's Green,' which is Audrey's solo. I mean, I would have liked to sing that, too, but I'm not about to tell Ms. Snowden how to do her job." Frannie wiped her nose on the sleeve of her fleece. "I'm a professional."

Whisper swerved closer.

"'Somewhere That's Green.' Never heard of it."

Frannie scoffed. "That's what people are going to say about me someday. *Frannie Vargas-Stein. Never heard of it.*"

Traffic was thick on Utility Street, so Frannie popped her bike onto the sidewalk and rode past store windows covered in ads for Hoke Week. *Must be nice,* she thought, feeling a teeny bit jealous of Silas Hoke's fame.

"Don't you think you're being a little dramatic?" Whisper asked.

"I'm trying to be a *lot* dramatic, but Miranda keeps stealing my spotlight! And why? Because of some fight we had, like, a thousand years ago."

"The famous fight." Whisper sighed. "I wish you'd tell me what—"

Frannie sped up to avoid the question. She hated reliving it. That kind of drama was too much, even for her.

The streets around the town square were blocked from traffic. Frannie and Whisper halted their bikes at the edge of the crowd. Over an ocean of bobbing heads, Frannie could make out a tower of wood and saw snaking tendrils of smoke. They were just in time for Hoke Week's opening ceremony: a fifteen-foot pyre of wood and kindling that she thought vaguely resembled a human. Once lit, people would file past and stoke it with sticks.

"Just like my future." Frannie sighed. "Up in smoke."

"You and your seized larynx have nothing to worry about," Whisper said. "You almost always score the lead."

"Yeah, well, *almost* always isn't going to cut it. The Camp Aria admissions office requires a current video of me in a lead role. And getting into Camp Aria is the only hope I have of becoming a serious actress."

"Puh-lease," Whisper said. "Pretty much no one in Hollywood went to Camp Aria."

"Yeah, and pretty much no one in Hollywood can act."

Frannie didn't mention the other reason she needed the lead in *Little Shop of Horrors*, the reason that had nothing to do with getting into an elite summer theater program nor with besting her ex-bestie. More than anything, it was about getting two hours of her parents' undivided attention.

For eleven years, Frannie's family life had been perfect, and then—plot twist!—Mom got pregnant with boys. Two of them!

Before Sami and Balthazar, Frannie got all the attention. And now? When Mom wasn't chasing the twins, she was working on her PhD. When Dad wasn't crisscrossing the country leading corporate sensitivity training seminars, *he* was chasing the twins so Mom could work on her PhD. Frannie went from being Baby Girl in the family to being Baby Can.

Baby, can you grab a diaper for Sami?

Baby, can you feed Balthazar?

Baby, can you turn down your music? The boys are napping.

It seemed Frannie had to be onstage to get her parents' attention. So she tried to make that happen as often as she could.

"Let's move closer to the front," Frannie said to Whisper, hoping the music from the old-timey brass band might distract her.

"I have to go," Whisper said, indicating her phone. "My dad and Tina are a few blocks over with the boys and want to meet up for a family dinner. Which will be hard, considering *we're not a family.*"

"Paisley too?"

"They want me to find her." Whisper peered into the crowd. "I'd rather play spin the bottle with Silas Hoke."

"Ew!" Frannie laughed. "That's so random."

"Yeah, well, so is a family dinner with people who aren't my family."

"What are you going to do?" Frannie asked, desperate for Whisper to stay.

"No way am I leaving you here alone." Whisper pulled her green beanie a little lower, as if to disguise herself. "I told them track practice was running late."

"That's the best news I've heard all day."

They rolled past souvenir booths and concession stands, pushing their way to the front of the crowd, where Mayor Chakrabarti, wielding a ceremonial torch, was taking his place at a podium. His usual flannel shirt and tie had been replaced with an old-fashioned black coat and a cap—a replica of the cap worn by Warden Cartwright, the man who pulled the switch on Silas Hoke.

"Ladies and gentlemen, residents and visitors, welcome to the opening ceremony of Misery Falls' Hoke Week Centennial!"

The crowd poked sticks at the stars and cheered.

"A century ago this Friday," the mayor continued, "Silas Hoke was electrocuted at the old Ashgate Prison, one block south. While I understand that many of our visitors want to take pictures in front of it, please do not enter. The structure is terribly unsafe, and"—the mayor lowered his voice—"tonight's guest of honor might still be in there. We here in Misery Falls think it's best to leave that tortured soul alone."

Frannie and Whisper exchanged a shuddering glance. Gemma, who was working at the store, and Sophie, who was at Photography Club—or was it peer tutoring?—were missing out.

"Ladies and gentlemen, what do you want me to do?"

"Light the fire!"

Mayor Chakrabarti teased the giant wooden pyre with his torch. "What's that?"

"Light the fire!"

"I can't hear you!"

"LIGHT THE FIRE!"

Mayor Chakrabarti held his torch to the pyre. As flames rolled upward, the crowd exploded into cheers. Frannie, who imagined herself bowing onstage whenever she heard applause, didn't let herself go there. If Miranda got the lead in *Little Shop of Horrors*, Frannie might never know the sound of an adoring audience again. Her only role would be that of Washed-up Actress. She was preparing.

"If this bonfire is supposed to represent Silas Hoke's electrocution, won't it make him madder?" Whisper asked. "And do we really want to make the vengeful ghost of a murderer madder?"

Boom!

Thunder cracked in the distance. Everyone screamed. The sky, previously filled with swirling colors and bright evening stars, turned dead black. The crowd became silent. So silent that Frannie could hear her pounding heart. The legend claimed that each year, on the anniversary of Silas Hoke's death, a Misery Falls girl vanished after a flash of lightning, so the thunder had everyone in a panic. But the lightning didn't come.

Until it did.

"Run!" Whisper urged.

Frannie saw a break in the crowd. They were beginning to pedal when suddenly Miranda, Zuzu, and Paisley stood before them, licking ice cream cones, too cool for fear.

Without a word, Whisper biked off in the other direction to avoid being caught in her track practice lie. But not Frannie. Leading ladies don't quit; they retire. And Frannie decided, in that moment, that she was far from retirement.

Another bolt of lightning.

Dogs barked, babies cried, and grown-ups clung to each other as everyone hurried to get away from Ashgate Prison before someone went missing.

Overcome with terror, Frannie made a sharp turn. Too sharp: her shin smacked painfully into a car's fender, and down she went onto the cold pavement.

Even colder now—rain began to fall. Legs everywhere started shuffling for cover. Frannie drew her own bloody legs up to avoid being trampled. One pair of legs, however, stayed put. She recognized the scar on that knee.

When she was eight, Frannie bought a pair of souvenir socks at the Hoke Stoke. Moments later, she'd noticed that a girl her age had slipped on a fallen scoop of ice cream and bloodied her knee. The girl was alone and crying, but no one could hear her above the cheers. So Frannie took her new Silas Socks, wrapped them around the girl's wound, and helped to find her parents. The girl's name was Miranda Young, and they'd declared themselves blood sisters for life.

Two years later, they were finished.

Now Miranda, Paisley, and Zuzu were standing above Frannie, watching *her* bleed. Didn't Miranda remember when she'd been in that position? Didn't she remember what Frannie had done for her?

Ka-sss!

"Did you seriously just take my picture?" Frannie asked.

"Don't worry, I'll post it so you can see," Miranda sneered. She dropped her ice cream by Frannie's feet, and she and Paisley began texting.

Click, clack, tick, tap.

"She does remember!" Frannie realized.

The rain got heavier. Miranda and Paisley took off, leaving Frannie to bleed out on the puddling pavement.

Oddly, Zuzu didn't follow. She just stood there, her designer clothes sticking to her skin.

"Costs a quarter to look at the freak," Frannie said.

Zuzu reached into her snakeskin bag and pulled out a package of silk Jōhin-brand handkerchiefs. She held it out to Frannie.

"What?"

Zuzu blew a bubble with her cinnamon gum. "Take it."

Pop!

Frannie looked up through the rain, too stunned to accept the offer. Or maybe she was too smart. Zuzu was one of *them*. It had to be a trap.

"They're limited edition," Zuzu said as she dropped the package in Frannie's bike basket. Then she took off after her friends, leaving behind the scent of Jōhin Classique and utter confusion.

Frannie opened the packet of handkerchiefs. The silks were soft, the jewel tone colors vibrant. So vibrant, in fact, that she didn't want to ruin them. She put them in her fleece pocket and let the rain take care of her scrape as the Hoke Stoke bonfire smoldered in the distance.

Zoop.

A text. Probably the photo Miranda took. Frannie swiped the screen, streaking beads of freshly fallen rain.

> ⚡ 💧 💧 💧 💧 🧽 **Meet at Crimson Creek Cemetery. 10pm Tuesday.**

A bolt of lightning, like those in the sky overhead? Drops of blood? A little coffin? There was no number attached. It had to be Gemma.

Frannie put her phone away, got on her bike, shook the rain from her face, and hurried for home. On the way, she passed two young girls holding hands. They looked to be the best of friends. And they probably were.

For now.

CHAPTER 6

GEMMA

Ten percent. That's how much Spirit Sanctuary customers saved on every purchase during Hoke Week. Now, Gemma was no mathlete, but didn't that come out to ten cents for every dollar? Hardly enough to justify missing the Hoke Stoke. Not that she had a choice. Thanks to the rain, the shop was packed tighter than a sage smudge bundle, and Gemma needed to prove herself. Another mishap and she'd be more fired than that giant pyre of logs in the town square.

Ever since she'd spilled the amethyst spheres, accidentally trashed a box of gemstones, and tangled thirteen dream catchers (a devil's dozen!), Gemma had been suffering from major job insecurity. The fact that the store was in the red—as her mom, Layla, and her aunt Harmony liked to say—didn't ease the pressure. Because this wasn't a nice ruby red. This was the almost-bankrupt kind of red. They counted on Hoke Week sales to keep the store going, yet Gemma was forbidden to sell, schedule, or basically touch anything.

Layla and Aunt Harmony swore that Gemma's job was just as important as her high school–age cousins' jobs. But was it? Luna took aura photographs, Brielle booked psychic readings, and Calli designed the window displays.

What did Gemma get to do?

On days like today, she stored wet umbrellas until customers were ready to leave. On dry days, she stocked shelves with astrology calendars, alphabetized books, and pulled broken pieces of incense from their jars. Baby jobs, in other words.

Meanwhile, Gemma was the only employee who, like Mom and Aunt Harmony, *believed* in the spirit world. When the moms were out of earshot, all the cousins did was make fun of customers and crack jokes.

Brielle: "Look at the astral planes on that guy."

Calli: "Call me Ouija, because I'm bored."

Luna: "How is Madam Vera a medium? She's more of a petite."

It wasn't only offensive; it was naive. Astral planes were like clubhouses for immaterial beings! Ouija boards were basically spirit cell phones! And say what you will about Madam Vera's height—she'd located fourteen missing pets in the last year alone!

But did the cousins ever get sent to the back office for disruptive behavior? No. They got promoted.

"Let me take that for you," Gemma offered to a damp gray-haired woman.

The woman handed over her umbrella, spilling rainwater down Gemma's macramé pants and into her clogs. "Thank you, little one."

Little one? It was a stab to the heart. Still, Gemma offered the woman a claim tag and an accommodating smile. Then, umbrella in hand, she hurried to fetch the mop before her mother noticed the wet floorboards.

Just as Gemma returned, Luna tap-tapped her on her shoulder.

"I need to conduct some lady business. Watch the register for a minute?"

"Can't." Gemma dragged the ropy head of the mop through the puddles, spreading them even more.

"Why? Are you too busy making the floor extra slippery so someone wipes out and sues us?"

"I'm not allowed," Gemma said, ignoring the dig.

Luna started doing the pee-pee dance. "It's fine, go ahead."

Gemma stopped mopping. "What do you mean, 'it's fine'? Did my mom say that?"

"Sure, yeah, go! Be right back."

Joy zinged up Gemma's spine. They were starting to trust her. Finally! She leaned the mop against the nearest wall, zigzagged around the soggy customers, and proudly positioned herself behind the old-fashioned steel-and-brass register.

Gemma's joy was quickly replaced by a thunderous rumble of pure power. Is this how Mayor Chakrabarti felt when he took the podium during the Hoke Stoke?

"Who's next?" she called.

First up was a blonde woman—crispy tan, bright eyes, tourist.

"I'm late for my Silas Hoke bus tour. Would you mind hurrying?" She placed a Reiki energy generator on the counter. "It's on sale. Thirty percent off."

Sale? The thunderous rumble of pure power inside Gemma dissolved into a whimpering mewl. Gemma had no idea how to ring up a sale item.

She glanced around the shop. Mom: reading auras. Aunt Harmony: demonstrating sound bowls. Luna: peeing. Brielle: selling crystals. Calli: leading a Kundalini prosperity chant. What choice did she have?

Picking up the Reiki energy generator, Gemma keyed in the price, subtracted half (30 percent was too hard to calculate), hit the Total button, and—Nothing. The register didn't budge. She tried it again. And again.

And again and again and again. The tourist sighed out a "Hurry" while tapping her fingers on the counter, as if Gemma had jammed the ancient machine on purpose. Other customers were shifting, muttering, and looking for someone more competent.

How many times had she told her mother that shops in the twenty-first century use card readers? But Layla Garrett insisted the antique register had an "occultish" charm. *How charming was it now, Layla?*

The tourist *tsk*ed. "Is there a manager you can call?"

Gemma smiled nervously. "Uh. Let me just . . ." She pounded the side of the register. Tugged at the bottom. Began punching random buttons.

"Young miss, the bus is going to leave without me!"

Young miss? That was even worse than *little one!*

Gemma found a disposable plastic knife, jammed it into the seam of the drawer, and . . . *Snap!* The knife broke in half, and Gemma stumbled backward into the most expensive item in the store: a statue of Ganesha, the four-armed, elephant-headed Hindu god of beginnings.

And endings, Gemma thought wretchedly as Ganesha took a header and shattered against the floor.

"Noooo!" Mom screeched as she hurried to the wreckage. She was wearing a floaty peasant blouse and

a sashaying hippie skirt, but there was nothing peace-and-love about her tone. "What are you doing behind the register?"

Gemma screwed her eyes shut as her mom apologized to the customer. Then came the tap of a single register button, followed by a musical *cha-king*. The ancient drawer yawned open just as a woman slipped on the water by the front door. She landed on her butt, and the mop landed on her.

Mom's face turned bankruptcy red. "I swear, Gemma. Every time I turn around, you're—"

Gemma took off. Another lecture on the hardships of being a single mother and a business owner was more than she could stand.

She barged into the back office. It was its usual wreck. Water-damaged books on faeries, broken amulets, burned-out gemstone display lights. And the smell: a heady bouquet of palo santo and failure.

Gemma sank into the chair, woke the stockroom computer, and googled *How to stop being pathetic*. There were 45,200,000 results—at least she wasn't alone. She closed the browser tab and saw her mother's inbox. Not only was Layla logged in; she had been in the middle of writing an email to Criss Borderlyne!

Gemma sat up.

Borderlyne was a permanently tanned, ab-sculpted, eyeliner-wearing ghost hunter whose spirit quest videos got millions of hits on YouTube. The waiting list for his Borderlyne Paranormal gear extended well into the afterlife. And now—could this be right? He was offering his latest product to the Spirit Sanctuary!

TO: Layla

SUBJECT: The Spirits Are Talking. Are You Listening?

Greetings Layla,

As you know, the Borderlyne G-Lens has helped millions of Questers track the electromagnetic patterns of ghosts. Now, with the affordable new G-Tone, paranormal fans like you can hear them! My patented wireless microphone employs ATDD functionality and a 350-millisecond FM sweep rate, so you'll never miss a message from your dearly departed again. It even translates the barks and mewls of deceased pets. Interested in purchasing a unit? I'm offering free overnight shipping while supplies last and will gladly charge the card you have on file.

Goose bumps covered Gemma's entire body.

It was a sign! A message from the spirit guides! Divine intervention!

Gemma had been begging her mother to get the G-Tone for months. Embracing technology (and a new cash register) was the only way the Spirit Sanctuary was going to stay relevant. But Layla always claimed she couldn't afford it.

And now the G-Tone was being offered by the creator himself. He even said it was affordable!

An idea hit Gemma like a second splash of umbrella water. Friday night would mark the one hundredth anniversary of Silas Hoke's electrocution. The town would be gathering outside of Ashgate Prison to banish his spirit for another year. But what if Silas didn't want to be banished? What if he had something to say to the fine folks of Misery Falls? And what if Gemma and her G-Tone were there, recording and posting it all? The Spirit Sanctuary would become famous overnight. Mom and Aunt Harmony would be out of the red and swimming in gold. And they'd owe it all to Gemma.

She scrolled to Layla's half-written reply.

TO: Mr. Borderlyne

SUBJECT: RE: The Spirits Are Talking. Are You Listening?

Dear Mr. Borderlyne, Thank you for your email but

That was as far as Mom got when, most likely, the storm hit and the Spirit Sanctuary got overrun, Gemma thought.

She gnawed her lip. Changing her mom's email reply was downright wrong. But hang on . . . She wasn't really *changing* it, was she? She was *finishing* it. Gemma leaned in and got to typing.

TO: Mr. Borderlyne

SUBJECT: RE: The Spirits Are Talking. Are You Listening?

Dear Mr. Borderlyne,

Thank you for your email but I'm way ahead of you. Please overnight one unit and charge it to my account. Thank you!

—Spirit Sanctuary

PS: I love your YouTube channel and your eyeliner. It's purple, right? The eyeliner, not the YouTube channel. Duh.

Gemma hit Send, then instantly trashed the email. By the time anyone figured out what she'd done, Mom and Aunt Harmony would be too busy counting their money to care.

Eager to tell the Grim Sleepers, Gemma dug out her phone and found several missed calls and texts from Sophie, Whisper, and, most recently, Frannie. All were demanding to know the meaning of *her* text. Gemma crinkled her forehead. She hadn't sent a text.

Down she scrolled—way down—until she found the message that had driven her friends into a frenzy. It had come from a BLOCKED NUMBER.

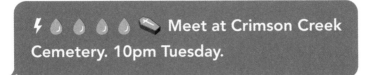

⚡ 💧 💧 💧 💧 🔪 **Meet at Crimson Creek Cemetery. 10pm Tuesday.**

Goose bumps returned to Gemma's skin, but not the excited kind. Crimson Creek Cemetery was where Silas Hoke had dragged Ginny Baker's severed leg and tried to attach it to himself. What if tonight's Hoke Stoke unleashed his spirit? What if he had finally found his way back and was on the hunt for a shiny new leg?

Now Gemma was extra glad she'd sent the email to Criss Borderlyne. If the G-Tone worked half as well as he claimed, she would have her answers soon enough.

CHAPTER 7

SILAS HOKE

The Hoke Stoke should be renamed.

I propose the Hoke Joke.

All that burning and cheering. It's barbaric. It's medieval. It's pointless.

Hoke Week was designed to empower the people of Misery Falls, to give them a sense of control. Make them think they can fight evil. Make them believe they can win.

But they can't.

Take the rain, for example.

All the planning in the world couldn't prevent nature from snuffing out their pitiful act of arson.

Well, I'm a force of nature, too.

I'm a storm.

My torrent descended upon this town once before—
one hundred years ago. The dragging noise of my wooden
leg was the thunder. The scream of my victim was the
shattering rain. The lightning, of course, was the electricity they used to kill me.

Which worked.

For a while, anyway.

Remember those four girls I've been watching? Whisper,
Sophie, Frannie, and Gemma? They remind me of Ginny
Baker and her little friends.

They thought they were so tough.

Funny, the wooden leg I killed Ginny with didn't
think she was tough at all.

Between the four of them, Whisper, Sophie, Frannie,
and Gemma have eight legs, eight arms, forty toes, forty
fingers, four noses, four tongues, and four heads.

By this time tomorrow night, I'll have plenty of parts
to choose from. Endless ways to make myself whole again.
A brand-new beginning.

The invitations have been sent.

Will they accept?

I hope so.

I mean, what have they got to lose?

Ha! Just ask Ginny Baker.

CHAPTER 8

WHISPER

It was time to get up, but slumber refused to loosen its tentacles on Whisper, trapping her inside a nightmare.

The town bonfire had grown into a Godzilla-size Silas Hoke, who was stomping all four members of the Grim Sleepers into four droplets of blood . . . just like the blood emojis in that mysterious text.

It was her father's early morning phone call that woke her up. She heard him pass her door, saying lawyery words like *settlement* and *discovery period*. His hushed tone meant it was Tuesday morning. Tuesdays were the worst. Because Tina, a psychiatrist, worked from home—Whisper's home. The *thrummm* of Tina's white noise machine meant she was with one of her patients, which meant everyone had to be dead silent.

"Sounds are grounds," Tina often reminded them.

"Grounds for *what*?" Whisper always asked, a reminder to Tina that her dorky catchphrase was incomplete without the words *for punishment*.

Beep. Beep. Beep.

Whisper patted her bedside table in search of her glasses, then silenced her alarm. Her bedroom door was open, and noise traveled quickly in their modern house. Something about too much marble and not enough carpet to absorb sound.

Sounds are grounds.

Wait. She sat up. Why was her bedroom door open? She hated open doors. Open doors made it easy for murderers to sneak inside and—

Murderer!

Her Hokezilla dream had distracted her from the real fright: yesterday's mysterious text about meeting at Crimson Creek Cemetery. Whisper checked her phone. At last, a reply from Gemma.

> I did NOT send that weird message! Someone or someTHING is messing with us. Don't worry, we'll know more tonight. I ordered something online. Tell u later.

Relief washed over Whisper. Scare was in the air during Hoke Week, and Gemma was obviously trying to milk it. That was all. End of story. Case closed. Class dismissed.

Whisper swung her feet off the bed, where they landed atop her fluffy slippers. She was about to slip them on when a clammy hand gripped her ankle and wrapped its reptilian fingers around her leg.

Someone screamed. A real eardrum-shattering, tooth-vibrating, five-alarm howler. It was Whisper, of course, but she was so scared, she felt disembodied. Like Ginny Baker! With a full-bodied electric-chair jolt, she ripped free of the cold grasp and ran downstairs like it was race day.

Then—*Slam.* A wall where there wasn't supposed to be a wall. A wall that smelled like blueberries, vanilla protein powder, nail polish, and entitlement.

From behind her askew glasses, Whisper caught the long, curved arc of Paisley's beloved phone sailing through the air, while Paisley's purple breakfast smoothie splashed all over her ivory sweater dress.

Then—*Smash.*

The phone struck the last hanging picture of Whisper's mother—a framed black-and-white shot of Jenny Martin at her bakery, licking chocolate cake batter from a mixing spoon. It fell from the pantry door and shattered.

Paisley's face went crimson. "What the—"

Whisper pointed at the stairs. "There's someone under my bed! We need to—"

Instead of the *thonk-thonk* of a one-legged maniac, Whisper heard the giggles of two fourth-grade boys.

Miles and Rayne.

Whisper felt herself go white as Paisley got redder, as though Paisley was Vincent the Vampire, draining Whisper's blood.

"The Hoke's on you!" Miles cried as he grabbed two lunch boxes from the fridge and tossed one to Rayne, who smiled idiotically through a cemetery row of half-missing teeth.

"Are you kidding me right now, Miles?" Whisper sputtered. "Why?!"

The boys clucked like chickens and flapped their arms. The clucks, however, were quickly overwhelmed by angry footsteps.

"Gotta go!" Miles said as he and Rayne raced to catch a bus that wasn't scheduled to arrive for another half hour.

"Who's the chicken now?!" Whisper shouted after them.

The footsteps gave way to Dad, in his business suit, pulling on his jacket and holding his car keys. His phone was still at his ear.

"I'm so sorry, Hiro. May I call you right back?"

James Martin slammed his phone on the kitchen counter and surveyed the crime scene. When he saw the photograph amid daggers of broken glass, his fiery anger turned ice-cold.

"Whisper. What did you do?"

"It wasn't my fault!"

Paisley's face became a mask of disbelief. "Really? Because the glass on the floor, the smoothie on my dress, and my cracked phone tell another story."

"Is this true?" James asked in that way that didn't require an answer. He already knew whom he believed, and it wasn't his daughter.

"She came in here raging like some kind of bucking matador!" Paisley accused.

"You mean bucking *bronco*?" Whisper corrected.

"Yes, actually. A wild bucking bronco. With rabies. And parvo."

Whisper stamped her foot. "I was being chased!"

"By two fourth graders!"

"I didn't know that! I thought it was—"

Another sharp *clap*—Tina's door slamming shut. She bounded into the kitchen, her sharp bob swinging alongside her clenched jaw. She had on the old gray cardigan she wore during therapy sessions, and the pinched scowl she wore everywhere else.

"Do you have any idea how all this screaming affects my clients?"

"It wasn't my fault," Whisper said again. "I thought Silas—"

Tina lifted a shushing finger to her thin lips. Then she whispered to James, "Accountability, remember?"

Dad sighed and glared. "Apologize, Willow."

Whisper's chest tightened. He *never* used her real name.

"And after you apologize, you can fix *this*." Paisley picked up her phone, her perfectly manicured nails flashing. "My screen is cracked."

"It was already cracked," Whisper said.

"*You're* cracked," Paisley said.

"If Whisper broke the screen, she'll pay for a new one," James said.

"*Seriously*, Dad?"

"And how about this dress?" Paisley pressed. "It's ruined."

Tina took a harder look at her daughter. "Is that my new Jōhin?"

Paisley rolled her eyes. "Mom, that's so not the point!"

Tina inhaled impatiently, nostrils flaring. "Your daughter has a real habit of blaming others, James."

"Why are you talking to *him*?" Whisper asked. "I'm right here!"

"I need to get to work." James gave Tina a kiss on the cheek. "Go back to your client. Willow will pay for the

dry cleaning and the broken phone, and we can put this whole thing behind us."

"What about the picture of Mom?" Whisper cried. "Why aren't you adding *that* to my bill? Don't you care about fixing *that*?"

The truth was, at that moment, Whisper wanted to snatch the photo of Jenny Martin from the shattered glass and tear it to pieces. This was all Mom's fault. If she were here, Tina wouldn't be—and Whisper would feel loved.

"Just apologize." Dad's kind brown eyes became hard and unfamiliar. "That's all I ask."

Whisper turned to Paisley, the last of all last-ditch options. "You *know* it was the boys' fault. Tell them. *Please*."

Paisley blink-blinked. For one second, Whisper saw a flicker of humanity. The flicker told her that Rayne had scared Paisley plenty of times in the past and that she knew the fear and embarrassment that came with it.

But the flicker was just that—gone like a spark and replaced by a hateful squint. "I don't know what you're talking about."

"If you can't even do that, I have no choice," James said. "You're grounded."

Paisley raised an eyebrow in victory.

"Dad, you're not listening to me! You never listen anymore!"

James gave her a disappointed look, held his phone to his ear, and walked out of the kitchen. Tina and Paisley followed, leaving Whisper alone to deal with the shattered glass and her broken heart.

And yet . . .

Being grounded *was* the perfect excuse to skip Gemma's trip to Crimson Creek Cemetery. But staying with these monsters was worse than whatever waited for her at the graveyard. Her home had become a haunted house, with Tina, Paisley, and Rayne bringing fresh horrors every day.

Sounds would *not* equal grounds. Whisper would risk it all and sneak out tonight. And if some deranged ghost was, in fact, at Crimson Creek waiting to saw Whisper's leg off, then maybe Paisley would finally apologize to *her*.

CHAPTER 9

FRANNIE

Frannie rocketed down the dark aisle toward the stage. Usually entering the school's theater intoxicated her—all the mysteries, the myths of showbusiness, and the promise of a captive audience's adoring eyes.

Today, however, Frannie just felt late. Whisper had caught her in the hall, upset about a picture of her mom she'd broken—or Paisley had broken, it was hard to tell. Frannie had done the best-friend thing and listened. Inside, though, she was freaking. A proper actor showed up *early* to do vocal warm-up tongue twisters. Ms. Snowden had taught them all the best ones.

Send toast to ten tense stout saints' ten tall tents!
Brisk brave brigadiers brandished broad bright blades!

Thirty-three thirsty thundering thoroughbreds thumped Mr. Thurber on Thursday!

Right then, Frannie didn't think she could say her own name. To be fair, Francine Wilhelmina Vargas-Stein was its own mouthful, but that wasn't the reason.

Ms. Snowden was about to announce the cast.

"You worry too much," Bubby Rose, Frannie's grandma, had said before Frannie left for school that morning. Easy for her to say! Bubby Rose had been a devastatingly gorgeous Broadway vamp in her day. Where had she been discovered? Camp Aria, that's where! The same program Frannie needed to be accepted into—or else.

Frannie arrived just as the first-period bell sounded, and sure enough, her beloved gray-haired drama director was late, too.

Into Frannie's imagination popped a horror scene too gory for any middle school play: Miranda Young making like Silas Hoke and sending Ms. Snowden to her grave— then stealing and modifying her cast list. It seemed plausible.

Or was it? For once, Miranda wasn't catting around, using her sinister powers to turn people against Frannie. Instead, she was typing away at her phone.

Click, clack, tick, tap.

The sounds made Frannie's bruises from the previous night's bike flop hurt even more. She could feel each

one of Miranda's taps like a poke right in her bruises' bluish centers.

Big blue bike bruises bring periodic pokes of pain.

Frannie could also see the vicious smirk on Miranda's face when she took that photo and shook it away.

"I bring news!" Zach Holt announced as he crossed the stage. Everyone stared at the eighth-grade piano player, who was referenced by both his first *and* last names. Hot guys often were.

Even Miranda glanced up from her phone.

"Ms. Snowden's mom busted her hip," he continued. "She went to Maine to take care of her. She'll be gone the whole semester."

Gasps!

Frannie struggled to comprehend. Ms. Snowden . . . gone? She envisioned the canceling of the musical, the rejection letter from Camp Aria, her future—working on Broadway as a street sweeper.

Zach Holt lifted Ms. Snowden's production binder above his head like it was Excalibur. "Guess what I found backstage?"

"Is the cast list in there?" Miranda asked.

"Indeed."

Twenty-two kids rushed the stage and circled Zach Holt like rabid hounds. Frannie was at the front of the pack, pouncing and clawing for the binder.

Crack. The sound of Frannie's jaws clapping together as someone elbowed her aside.

"Got it!" Miranda cried.

Frannie jammed her hand into the back pocket of her striped overalls. Inside were the jewel tone silk handkerchiefs Zuzu had given her. It was just a year ago that Frannie had given up her baby blankie, Murphy. Only the Grim Sleepers knew. Secretly, she still missed Murphy, and she'd found that the Jōhin handkerchiefs soothed her in a similar way. But no amount of silk could ease *this* tension.

"Audrey . . . " Miranda said numbly.

Frannie's heart skittered around in her chest.

Miranda looked up and said, in soft disbelief, "Audrey. Me." Then a squeal. *"I'm playing Audrey!"*

Frannie strangled the Jōhin silks.

The stage exploded into congratulatory cheers and jealous mutters. Miranda dropped the binder—she was too good for it now—and the wannabe cast dove after it like pigeons after breadcrumbs. People began shouting out who got which roles.

Frannie didn't hear them. The world sounded like it was underwater. And yet she was still able to hear Zach Holt say, "Congrats, Frannie, you got the Audrey understudy."

Congrats? *Congrats?* She'd be playing Sunday matinees for nursing home oldies—if she was lucky. Miranda would never let her live it down. Tears pressed at her eyes as she imagined telling Bubby Rose the devastating news.

Suddenly a husky female voice rang out.

"Players! Performers! Pantomimists alike! Your director has arrived!"

Director?

Through a blur of tears, Frannie watched a young redheaded woman dressed in black bell-bottoms, a black turtleneck, and black-framed glasses move toward them with soft but commanding panther-like steps.

"Good morrow, as Shakespeare would say. My name is DayNa—capital *D*, lowercase *A*, lowercase *Y*, capital *N*, lowercase *A*. No last names on my stage, please. We assume the names of our characters, not our ancestors."

Frannie liked her already.

DayNa motioned for Zach Holt and the pigeons to step down and take their seats. Once they were gone, she padded up the steps and took center stage. "You might recognize me from my off-off-Broadway one-woman show *A Streetcar Named DayNa*, or from my follow-up *A Long DayNa's Journey into Night*. Impressive, yes. But those shows didn't magically appear. I worked hard to make them happen, and Cynthia Snowden, my mentor, helped me every step of the way. So when I received word that she needed a substitute director, I said, 'Put me in,

Coach. Let me sprinkle a little San Francisco spice into this production!' And she did."

While everyone applauded politely, Frannie folded her arms across her chest and blinked back tears. Maybe DayNa was happy being a substitute, but FranNie was not.

"While my background is more in, shall we say, *experimental* theater, I am certainly qualified for"—she waved an arm around as if clearing a cloud of smoke—"this. No matter the play, the most important thing you can do is *listen*. Hear your scene partner's lines for the first time, every time. Only then will your character be able to find an appropriate reaction." She paused, allowing her words to penetrate. "Is one of your fellow players speaking? Listen, then react. Did someone flub a line? Listen, then react! Did a bored audience member just yawn?" She held a hand to her ear.

"Listen, then react!" everyone answered.

"No!" DayNa grinned. "Kick their butt after the show!"

Everyone laughed. Frannie couldn't help but smile. Maybe, just maybe, there was life after understudy-dom. If Frannie could get a good video of herself during the nursing home show, maybe Camp Aria—

A photo popped up on the giant screen above the stage, giving way to more laughter.

Huh?

It was a picture of Frannie. At the Hoke Stoke. On the wet pavement, pretzeled around her bike, knee bleeding and face clenched like she was holding in a poo. Miranda had taken that picture. And now she'd posted it.

DayNa wasn't listening *or* reacting. She kept rattling on about her directing philosophies until she finally noticed all the upward gazes.

"Is that you, Overalls?" she asked.

Frannie nodded, ashamed.

If only she were the kind of girl who could stand up and give a viral-worthy speech about resilience. About how bullies can't bring her down. About how she's her own best friend and doesn't care what Miranda thinks of her. Instead, Frannie felt tiny and insignificant. Exhausted and lonely. Nothing but a bruised, used, and abused Baby Can.

"Do you know how that photo got there?" DayNa asked her.

Frannie tugged a loose thread on her shirt. "I have an idea."

"Would you like to share it with us?"

"Not really."

"Why?"

"Because I'm tired of fighting."

"Then take a nap," Miranda muttered.

DayNa ignored Miranda, choosing to stay with Frannie instead. "How would you describe that feeling in one word?"

Frannie shrugged. She was too tired to answer questions.

"Fill in the blank," DayNa pressed. She was standing directly over Frannie now, her green eyes beaming compassion. "Right this second, I feeeeeeel . . ."

The theater became silent, the cast members still. Everyone was waiting for Frannie's word, in the same the way that *Wicked* audiences wait for the crescendo in "Defying Gravity"—like their next breath was tied to it. Frannie had a choice to make: shrug again or claim her solo.

She lifted her gaze. "Hopeless. Right now, I feel hopeless."

Then DayNa did the oddest thing. She began slow-clapping. "What's your name?"

"Frannie?"

DayNa leafed through Ms. Snowden's binder, stopped on a page, and nodded. "Frannie, you're playing Audrey."

"Audrey's *understudy*," Miranda corrected. "*I'm* the lead."

"No, Melinda, you have it backward."

"It's Miranda, and no, I don't. It says right there that—"

DayNa closed the binder gently, but it felt like she'd slammed it. "That was *Ms. Snowden's* casting decision. This is mine."

"Based on what?" Miranda dared. "You didn't even hear us audition."

"Oh, but I did. I listened and reacted."

"To what?"

"To the song in Frannie's soul. I listened to a girl who feels hopeless and wronged. A girl who thinks she is treated so unfairly, she's ready to give up. And that, my dear thespians, is *exactly* how Audrey feels when our story begins. Frannie will play Audrey because Frannie *is* Audrey."

"I don't have to *be* the character to *play* the character," Miranda protested. "It's called acting!"

"Then *act* like a good sport and congratulate Frannie on her starring role."

Frannie's hands flew to her mouth, Oscar-winner style. Glancing around, she wondered if others heard that, too. They had! Some patted her on the back, others gave her thumbs-ups, and everyone, even Zach Holt, said she deserved it.

Except Miranda, who was arguing with DayNa and threatening to sue.

Amid the chaos, Frannie peered up at the giant screen and grinned. It might not have been the most flattering photo, but it had officially become her favorite.

CHAPTER 10

SOPHIE

To Sophie, failing, or the threat of failing, felt a lot like skydiving. Not that she had tried skydiving. Failing at that would suck. It was more about the sensation. Soaring through the air, not sure where or when she would land. Surrendering, letting go, opening up to the unknown. Because when a girl sticks to schedules and to-do lists and does precisely what must be done to get a perfect grade, there aren't a lot of unknowns.

Except on Tuesday afternoons at JAM.

The Julian Academy of Music was the one place where Sophie *wanted* perfection—and the one place that made her feel like she was crashing into a tree.

All.

The.

Time.

"Sorry I'm late," she told Ms. Drassel, her hair dripping wet. "I couldn't get a ride after school." All right, that was a bit of a lie. She could have gotten a ride from Frannie's mom, but Sophie needed her ten thousand steps.

"Understandable," Ms. Drassel said. She had a slight accent that Sophie had never managed to place. "I wouldn't let you in my car looking like that, either. Did you just come from PE?"

Sophie wanted to say her hair was soaked with rain, not sweat, but why bother? Ms. Drassel despised excuses even more than tardiness. Tall and lithe with a pencil's posture and frown lines that spoke to her chronic disappointment, the old woman was not to be messed with.

"I'm sorry, it won't happen again."

Sophie took her seat at the piano and inhaled sharply, breathing in the lemony scent of wood polish and the sticky sweetness of gummy bears, which were there to keep the younger kids motivated. Not that Sophie would ever eat those. Sugar, gelatin, and dyes were unhealthy. And she didn't need gummy bears as a reason to go to JAM. She didn't need any reason at all.

Sophie loved piano. It transported her to an alternate reality where spelling and grammar didn't count.

It didn't hurt that Jade, for all her skills, had never played an instrument. Not a violin. Not a bagpipe. Not an accordion, a gong, nor a recorder. Not even a stereo. Music was the only thing Sophie could claim for herself. To her, the eighty-eight keys on a piano were actual keys that unlocked eighty-eight places to chill.

"Sophie, are you serious about piano?" Ms. Drassel rolled up the sleeves on her signature white dress shirt. She wore one all the time, along with poppy-red lipstick that often bled into the tiny lines around her lips.

"Very, Ms. Drassel."

Which was mostly true. Sophie *was* serious about piano—serious about not taking it too seriously. Serious about enjoying it.

"I'm serious too," Ms. Drassel said, "and I have a ten-month waiting list to prove it. If you can't make it here on time, I'll find someone who can."

The idea made Sophie wilt. Being around Ms. Drassel was exciting. Her sharp birdlike features were framed by a plume of silver hair that might have been styled by a head-on wind. Her denim was crisp, her flats velvet, and her floral perfume expensive. Aside from Ms. Drassel's fingernails, which were short, buffed, and polish free, she was pure prestige.

Meanwhile, Sophie, in her black hoodie, white jeans, and black rain boots, looked like a soggy Oreo. "I want to be here," she said. "I promise."

"Prove it." Ms. Drassel took her yardstick and placed it behind Sophie's back to align her posture. "Today you will be playing Camille Saint-Saëns's *Danse Macabre*."

Sophie wiggled her fingers and began.

Ms. Drassel took her usual seat on the sofa and set the metronome. Above her head, a horizontal window bordered the adjacent studio—*his* studio. Sophie tried her hardest not to look.

Six months earlier, Sophie had been right here, playing Tchaikovsky, when she spotted a slightly older boy strumming the guitar through that window. As if sensing her, he'd glanced up, locked eyes with her, and grinned.

Sophie—who never grinned at boys, especially slightly older ones—had grinned back. And just like that, they were . . .

What? Sophie wasn't sure. Guitar Guy—the only name she had for him—seemed to delight in distracting her with goofy faces and occasional glances, which chopped up her Chopin, turned her Mendelssohn into Mendel*slop*, and made Ms. Drassel boil.

Sophie had mentioned Guitar Guy to her friends. They, of course, bombarded her with Relax Attacks and urged her to take a risk for once and talk to him. Except Gemma, of course, who considered boys a distraction from more important things like scary stories and astral planes.

With his dark hair (blond streak in the front), old concert T-shirts, and black nail polish, Guitar Guy was one more reason that going to JAM was easy. But the focusing part? That was hard.

Now, after forty seconds and only one *tsk*, Sophie detected a light *thup* against the window.

She wanted to look.

Instead, she told herself to focus. Begged herself to focus. Soon she was focusing so hard on focusing that it became hard to focus. *Focus, Sophie! Focus!*

Thup. Thup.

Sophie's hands began to betray her. Her wrists: too tight. Her fingertips: not striking with the right bounce.

Thup. Thup. Thup. Thup.

Almost done. But her clammy hands, those gentle *thup*s, the promise of another grin . . .

Focus, Sophie! Focus!

She was almost there. Then, on the final page of music, Sophie struck a chord badly enough to wake the dead.

"Ssss." The sound of Ms. Drassel's hiss.

Sophie fumbled again and lifted her hands. If playing piano was like skydiving, then she'd just crash-landed on a busy highway. She stared at the piano keys. Now they looked like eighty-eight gnashing teeth.

Without music, the next window tap was a whole lot louder.

THUP.

Sophie couldn't help it. She looked. So did Ms. Drassel.

The window was covered in sticky gummy bears.

Sophie didn't expect this and couldn't help it: she giggled.

"That *boy!*" Ms. Drassel lowered the window's blinds. "Today's lesson is over. And you will be too, Ms. Wexler, unless you get your priorities straight."

With that, Ms. Drassel swung her leather tote over her shoulder and glided from the room, leaving Sophie alone in a cloud of shame and expensive floral perfume.

Then—*Ping.*

A text. Had Ms. Drassel called her parents already?

Praying this wasn't her last visit to JAM, Sophie nervously tapped on her screen.

It wasn't her angry parents. It was a GIF of a gummy bear, and contact information for someone named Dane Jeremy.

Was Guitar Guy's name Dane Jeremy? Did Dane Jeremy just AirDrop his contact information to Sophie's phone? Was this seriously happening?

Yes, yes, and yes!

Teeming with adrenaline and unsure what to do next, Sophie sprang from the piano bench, grabbed her bag, and hurried for the exit. She ran into the rain, skipped down the sidewalk, and jumped in puddles. She got water in her boots and mud on her jeans. Maybe music wasn't the only way to feel free.

Dane Jeremy AirDropped me!

Then, *Splash!*

Sophie hadn't wanted it, she certainly hadn't expected it, and she had no idea what would come of it. It felt dangerous. Uncertain. Exhilarating. Like she was standing at the open door of an airplane. Ready to jump, ready to free-fall, ready to soar! So what if it was just a text?

Skydive, AirDrop . . . Same thing.

GEMMA

Gemma yanked open the shop's door with a flourish, inhaled the powdery tang of incense, and then exhaled through her nostrils like a charging bull. Tonight's mission: pick up the Borderlyne G-Tone undetected, speed-read the manual, and take the G-Tone to Crimson Creek Cemetery so she could contact whomever—or whatever—had summoned the Grim Sleepers.

Once she'd captured the voice of this tech-savvy spirit, Gemma—Cinderella of the Spirit Sanctuary— would become Gemma, Dialoguer of the Dead! Forget doing readings like Madam Vera; Gemma would have her own YouTube Channel, like Criss Borderlyne. She'd fire her cousins and hire—

"What brings you here?" her mother asked. She stood at the door of the Spirit Sanctuary, arms crossed, foot tapping. Gemma had Tuesdays off from work, so it was a fair question. But there was something more to her mom's tone: a quiet confidence that suggested she already knew the answer.

"What wouldn't bring me here? We live upstairs, and I work here. So."

"I assumed you and the girls would be at the Hoke Poke."

"Yeah, we're going a little later. Jade, Sophie's sister, is going to take us," Gemma lied. Because *We're skipping the blood drive so we have enough energy to get to the cemetery and meet a mysterious texter who may or may not be Silas Hoke* probably wouldn't fly.

"I'm just here to pick up a little package I had delivered. I'll check the office and get out of your—"

"Office?"

This came from Aunt Harmony, who'd stepped away from a customer to interject. She was gripping a Día de los Muertos candle like a bludgeon. "Oh, honey, your package is *not* in the office."

Why was everyone acting so weird? Maybe they were possessed. All the more reason to grab that G-Tone and put it to work.

"Where is it?" Gemma asked breezily.

"In the alley."

"The *alley*? Why?"

"The crate didn't fit in the store."

Gemma drew back her head. "Crate?"

"Crate," her mother and aunt Harmony said together.

"That's not mine," Gemma assured them. "My package is small."

Layla and Aunt Harmony exchanged a look.

Gemma's skin began to prickle. "What's going on?"

Layla's amusement hardened.

"Yesterday evening, when you snuck onto my email," she began.

Uh-oh.

". . . and used my credit card . . ."

Oh no.

"You didn't order a single G-Tone. You ordered a single *unit* of G-Tones."

Gemma swallowed. "How many are in a *unit*?"

She could almost hear the whistle of the bomb dropping.

"One hundred," Layla said.

Boom.

Gemma's legs felt wobbly. She leaned against the doorjamb for support as the interior of the store spun. Wicca blended with voodoo, occult with Reiki.

"I'll—I'll fix it," Gemma stammered. "I'll email him. I'll return them—"

"We tried," Aunt Harmony snipped. "Clearance sale, Gemma. No returns. You didn't read the sales agreement."

Gemma gripped her roiling stomach.

"So, here's what we're going to do," her mother said. "You're going to work in the shop until every one of those useless pieces of junk is paid off. Whatever plans you have for the next several years? Cancel them. Life as you know it is over."

Instead of running off the way she did after breaking the Ganesha statue, Gemma stood firm. She was used to being the only believer in the room.

"Punish me all you want, but the G-Tone is not a useless piece of junk."

Layla threw a nervous look at their customers. "Keep your voice down."

"I'm trying to make this place cool, Mom. It's not the 1800s. No one wants old-fashioned cash registers and dusty old moon-goddess capes! They want technology."

A middle-aged woman holding a dusty old moon-goddess cape returned it to the rack.

Aunt Harmony hurried for the shopper. "Excuse my niece. She's upset. I assure you, those capes are not dusty."

Layla leaned into Gemma and, through clenched teeth, said, "Tell your friends you won't be joining them at the Hoke Poke, and go deal with that crate."

"Fine," Gemma snarled. "You can silence me, but you can't silence the dead! The G-Tone is going to prove it!"

In the alley, a crate as tall as Gemma waited by the dumpster. It was branded with the Borderlyne Paranormal logo.

Gemma ripped open the crate. Inside were boxes, each with a white label that read: G-TONE ATDD/350 FM (1). The technical jargon filled her with confidence. When she returned with a trove of ghost gossip, everyone in Misery Falls, including her family, would finally take her seriously.

Fired up with conviction, Gemma grabbed a G-Tone and took off. It was getting late. She had a graveyard to get to and Silas Hoke to record.

CHAPTER 12

SILAS HOKE

Can hearts salivate? Because mine is dripping with anticipation.

Everything is set. The cemetery is ready to receive. Now I wait.

And wait.

Twenty-seven minutes left.

How fitting. Twenty-seven. The cursed number twenty-seven.

Kurt Cobain. Janis Joplin. Amy Winehouse. Jimi Hendrix.

All died at age twenty-seven.

And those are just a few musicians.

There are more.

Lots more. Even a few who died at, oh, let's say . . . age twelve.

But I'm too restless to name them. Too anxious. Too excited.

Twenty-six minutes.

I'm not a very patient person.

Ha! Did I say *person*? Old habits die hard. Really hard, in my case.

Twenty-five minutes.

The girls are gathering outside the home of the one called Whisper.

That's where I am, too.

What? Did you think I was waiting at the cemetery? And miss my chance to watch the fear in these girls' faces deepen with every step?

Twenty-four minutes.

First: the one called Sophie arrives. Naturally. She's the studious one. The one feeling pressure from her older sister, Jade. Don't worry, Sophie. The sibling rivalry is almost over. Soon Jade will be an only child.

Second: the one called Frannie. Too cold for that skirt, Frannie—I can see your bruised knee from that unfortunate spill at the Hoke Stoke. You probably still think Miranda is your biggest threat. Fool. I'm your biggest threat now.

Third: the one called Gemma. Look at her stride. Full of confidence tonight, aren't we? She's holding some kind of weapon. Will you be aiming that in my direction, Blondie? Only if you see me first!

Finally: the one called Whisper slips from her darkened doorstep. She's the one who's always complaining about her dad's girlfriend and her kids. Their house will be so much more quiet and peaceful once Whisper has vanished.

They're off.

Fifteen minutes till the party begins.

I stay a block ahead of them. It's easy. I know the route they'll take. Down Hemlock Lane. Over to Raven Boulevard. Straight along Moss Street. They'll avoid downtown so they don't run into any tattletales on Hoke Poke night.

A pity. People might have had a chance to save them.

Ten minutes.

Oh look. They're approaching old Ashgate Prison.

Five minutes.

Ashgate. They remember what happened there, don't they? I sure do.

Fear is overtaking their faces. They're moving slower. Clutching one another. Waving their flashlights through the darkness like rescue workers. Even Gemma looks scared.

I need to get closer.

I need to taste their terror.

Yes! We're almost there.

Ready or not, girls, here I come.

WHISPER

Whisper's breath hitched. "What was that?" She lowered her black beanie. *I can always run,* she told herself. *If things get too scary, I can always run. I am a record breaker. I am speed.*

The rain had stopped, but the sky remained as black as an undertaker's suit. Even the moon was afraid to show itself.

"Someone must have stepped on a twig," Gemma said to the control panel on her G-Tone. She was walking, talking, and fidgeting, determined to make it work.

"I heard it too," Frannie said. "It sounded like footsteps."

"Because we have feet and are taking steps," Gemma told them.

Whisper looked behind them. Just an empty street. The local shops had closed early, and everyone was downtown for the Hoke Poke. At least, Whisper *hoped* everyone was downtown. She couldn't shake the feeling that someone was following them.

"Me gusta leer. Correr. La goma. El cuaderno. La educación es muy fácil," Sophie muttered.

"Soph," Whisper whispered. Even her voice was hiding. "You have to stop that!"

"And what? Fail my Spanish vocab quiz tomorrow?"

"Would you rather fail a quiz or fail at being alive?" Frannie asked.

"How is studying Spanish going to get me killed?"

"Because I'm going to kill you if you don't stop mumbling," Frannie teased. "You sound possessed."

"And I'm trying to listen for footsteps," Whisper added. "I swear I heard someone by the prison."

Gemma shook the G-Tone, which hadn't lit up once. "There weren't any footsteps."

"Then what was that scuttling sound?"

"The land crab of Misery Falls," Frannie said in a semidecent Transylvanian accent.

"You mean Tina?"

"Maybe she knows you snuck out," Sophie said, "and she's looking for you."

"Ha! That land crab would *not* come looking for me," Whisper scoffed.

Sneaking out had been easier than Whisper imagined. All she had to do was creep into Tina's office and blast the white noise machine to cover her tracks. By the time Tina turned it off, Whisper was gone. But as they inched down Moss Street, Whisper was kind of wishing she'd been caught and sent back to her room.

The other girls hadn't had any trouble, either. Sophie's parents were giving blood at the Hoke Poke, then going to a post-poke party. Frannie had said she'd have a late night building sets for the play and had arranged a ride home. And Gemma had just taken off, knowing the store was busy and her mother would be working late. Was it risky? Absolutely. But no riskier than meeting a mysterious texter who may or may not be a dead murderer at a CEMETERY!

The trees were getting thicker now, taller. Their branches swayed in slow motion, shedding leaves like giant tears. The houses in this part of town were older, the fences pointier. The road ahead curved into darkness, like a tongue down a black throat. Were they really doing this?

SKRONG! SKRONG!

The G-Tone emitted an actual *tone*, like a church bell filtered through an old-timey video game. Its lights flared to life.

The girls screamed and clustered.

"Who's here?" Frannie asked, waving her flashlight.

Can we please run? Whisper thought. She was shaking too hard to speak.

"¡Dios mío!" Sophie cried, returning to Spanish mode.

Gemma's attention remained fixed on the G-Tone, her blue eyes going purple in its red flash. How was she not terrified? Unless . . .

"Aha!" Whisper narrowed her eyes. "I *knew* you sent that text!"

Gemma looked up. "What? Why would I do that?"

"So you could spook us with your G-Touch!"

"G-*Tone*," Gemma corrected, "and no, it wasn't me." Her eyes were darting, her voice pinched. Like maybe she wished it *had* been her.

"What does that light mean?" Sophie asked, teeth chattering. "Is *he* here?"

Gemma thrust a hand into her pocket and dislodged her forbidden phone. The G-Tone instruction manual was online, so an exception could be made. "It means . . . It means . . ." She hung her head. "It means I forgot to charge it."

They loosened their grip on one another and gigglesighed with relief.

"Onward," Gemma said, disappointed.

(She was the only one.)

They hadn't made it half a block when the sounds of footsteps returned.

Whisper stopped. Her swallow went down like a fishhook. "Not a twig."

"It's your imagination," Gemma said. "Everything is fine."

"In horror movies the person who thinks everything is fine always gets killed."

"Why are we doing this, anyway?" Frannie said, suddenly clueing into the fact that this was one of the dumbest, most irresponsible things a girl (or four) could do.

Gemma stopped and looked at them squarely. "Truth?"

They nodded.

"Because it's scary how unscary this club has become," she said. "We don't sleep with the lights on or zip our sleeping bags together anymore. We've become G-rated. And not in a good way. Our G used to stand for *Guts, Gore, Grim,* or *Gross.* Now it's just *Goofy, Goody-goody, Giggly,* and *Gathetic.*"

They exchanged looks and then busted out laughing. Even Gemma, who was trying to sound serious,

had to smile at *gathetic*. But joking aside, she was right. Somewhere along the way, the Grim Sleepers had lost their edge. They'd stopped riding the wild rapids of fear, stopped clinging to courage; they were drifting down a lazy river of shared history and old traditions. The wild waves were gone. Their ride was flat.

"I'm with Gemma," Sophie said. "I've been playing it safe for too long. I mean, we all have."

"Agreed," Frannie said. "But if I get murdered and can't play Audrey, I'll haunt you."

"I agree too," Whisper said, meaning it. The club made her feel like she belonged to something special. Yes, saving the environment and being on the track team were important—super important—but those came to her naturally. Bravery was something Whisper had to work for. When she summoned it, she felt the kind of power one can't feel from a first-place trophy. Trophy power was fleeting, but facing-a-fear power lasts a lifetime. So did great friends. "We're the Grim Sleepers, not the *Prim* Sleepers," she bellowed. "Let's do this!"

"Yes!" Gemma said. "And don't worry, we're being watched by angels and protected by guardians." She pointed at the dark sky. "They'll look out for us."

The Grim Sleepers looked at her blankly. Always wanting to believe, but never quite sure.

"Besides," Gemma said, changing strategies. "Don't you want to find out who sent that text?"

"I am not afraid," Frannie said.

Whisper cocked her head. "Not even a little bit?"

"I am not afraid."

"Like, not at all?" Sophie asked.

"I am not afraid."

"Frannie, what's happening right now?" Gemma asked, afraid. "Are you glitching?"

"It's an old acting exercise. You repeat a sentence that's not believable until you believe it. It works. Try it."

"I am not afraid," Gemma said.

"I am not afraid," Sophie said.

Whisper took a shallow breath. It felt like a tentacle was wrapped around her ribs, squeezing. "I am not afraid."

"I am not afraid."

"I am not afraid."

"I am not afraid."

"I am not afraid."

Each time a girl said it, the phrase got sharper; a word hatchet chipping away at their collective fear. As they ambled down the block, arms linked and chanting, Whisper thought of *The Wizard of Oz*, and how Dorothy clung to the Scarecrow, the Tin Man, and the Lion. Only, this wasn't a Technicolor dreamland, and

lions, tigers, and bears were the least of her concerns. *I am not afraid.*

"I am not afraid."

"I am not afraid."

"I am not afraid."

Down the hill they went, all in a line, sinking into the night as though it were a midnight ocean.

"I am not afraid."

"I am not afraid."

"I am not afraid."

Empowering as it was, their chant began to wither as the gnarled wrought iron gates that lorded over the Crimson Creek Cemetery came into view.

"We can't get in." Whisper indicated a chain and a padlock that hung from the entry.

Ignoring her, Gemma climbed to the top of the gate and jumped over, followed by Sophie and then Frannie, who extended a helping hand so Whisper couldn't chicken out.

"I am not afraid," Whisper muttered as she climbed. "I am not"—she jumped and landed firmly on the wet earth—"afraid."

Ancient headstones jutted like broken teeth from a jawbone. Towering oaks grasped downward with spindly fingers. The actual Crimson Creek, hidden by a pelt of forest, growled like a wolf. *I am afraid!*

"Look," Gemma said, pointing at a faraway spot of light pulsating in the gloom.

Frannie aimed her flashlight. The beam hit fog like it was a pane of glass.

"Hello?" Gemma called.

No one answered.

Whisper's heart pounded against her chest as if trying to escape.

"Do you think that's his grave?" Sophie managed.

"There's only one way to find out," Gemma said, dragging them forward.

"Actually," Whisper tried, "we could download a map of the cemetery and—"

"Shhhhhh!"

With arms linked and mouths too dry to speak, the Grim Sleepers crept silently through the fog and closer to the light.

"It's a lantern," Sophie said.

Centered atop a small rectangular stone that was cracked nearly in half was a lantern. It illuminated one hundred years of graffiti: ROTTEN AND FORGOTTEN, MAGGOT FOOD, REST IN PIECES. The name of the grave's occupant, though, was still visible.

SILAS HOKE

Whisper's stomach lurched. She saw black sunbursts. Was Silas Hoke really in there? Was he that close?

They'd gathered around the narrow plot of land and were looking down at the overgrown weeds, tempted to run, daring to stay, when—

Thonk-thonk.

The girls bristled.

Thonk-thonk.

Gemma turned to the others, her mouth open but unable to speak.

"Wooden," Frannie whimpered, "leg."

Lightning flashed, hurling shadows from cemetery crosses and mausoleum angels and illuminating the terrified expressions of the four girls.

"Ahhhhh!" they all shouted.

And then four corpses fell from a nearby tree.

"Run!" Frannie yelled. Or was it Sophie? Maybe it was Gemma. Whisper's ears were ringing too loudly to be sure.

Everyone took off.

Whisper remained.

It was as if her limbs were made of coffins and her torso were a tombstone—it was *that* impossible to move. She told her legs to be brave, begged them to find courage, urged them to go.

For the first time *ever*, they refused.

CHAPTER 14

SILAS HOKE

Look at them run. All in different directions. The dramatic one's still screaming, "I'm not afraid!"

Oh, I think she's very afraid.

Whisper is still here. Standing above my grave. Petrified as a tree. Beanie pulled over her glasses.

I step out from the shadows.

Walk straight toward her.

I stand one foot away, scrutinizing this frightened creature.

Maybe she's the type who wants to get it over with.

So do I, Whisper. So do I.

I hear a *sniff-sniff.*

Is she crying?

No, I don't see tears.

Sniff-sniff. Sniff-sniff.

Aha. She's picked up my scent.

My very specific scent.

Not of half-eaten corpses.

Not of decayed flesh.

Not of electrified organs.

But the distinctive smell of—

CHAPTER 15

ZUZU

"Jōhin Classique and cinnamon gum?" Whisper asked. She rolled back the edge of her beanie just enough to see who was standing in front of her. "Zuzu? What are you doing here?" Whisper's pupils were wide. Her voice was raspy. "Four bodies! It's not safe! We have to go!" Her legs didn't move. She was in shock.

"It's fine, Whisper. You're safe," Zuzu assured her. She even smiled a little to prove it.

"No! You don't get it!" Whisper pointed at the pile of corpses under the tree. "See?"

"I know." Zuzu blew a cinnamon-scented bubble. "I did that."

Pop!

Whisper took a step back. "*You* killed them?"

"No!" Zuzu laughed. She knew this was going to be fun. "They're not real. I was trying to scare you."

Whisper drew back her head. Her expression screwed into a twist of confusion and hurt. "Why would you want to do that?" Then—"Wait! Did Gemma put you up to this?"

"No!" Zuzu said, offended. She was perfectly capable of terrifying people on her own, thank you very much.

"Paisley and Miranda, then. They're hiding behind a gravestone, shooting a video, aren't they?"

"No, it was just me—"

"Shhhh." Whisper cupped her ear.

Everything inside Zuzu began to rev. Were things about to get dangerous? "What is it?"

"I'm trying to hear it."

"Hear what?"

"Their texting," Whisper said. *"Click, clack, tick, tap."*

Zuzu's revving insides slowed. She knew those sounds well. "I'm only one here. I promise. Aside from *them*." She indicated the buried bodies, of which there were hundreds.

"This was all you?" Whisper asked. "Really?"

Exhilaration zipped up Zuzu's spine. She'd finally exposed a tiny piece of herself, and no one had made fun of her. It was an encouraging sign. Perhaps, in time, she could reveal more.

"How did you do all this?" Whisper asked, just like Zuzu had hoped she would.

Zuzu was proud of her ingenuity and longed for someone to appreciate it. Someone *alive*. Hiding her dark side was lonely. After years of scaring in solitude, Zuzu craved likeminded friends. She wanted to share the shadows.

"They're mannequins."

Whisper stepped closer to the lifeless heap. "Where did you get them?"

"My parents own Jōhin. Our garage is full of them."

"Duh," Whisper said with a deprecating eye roll.

Zuzu held the lantern above her work. "The blood around their mouths is made from corn syrup, a dash of cocoa powder, a few drops of food coloring, and a sprinkle of orange peel shavings. That's how I got that nice scabby texture."

"And the dangling eyeball?"

"Gelatin. I melt and mold it in my basement."

"The exposed neck bones?"

"Tissue paper over eyelash glue. I use Jōhin Risqué Lash Adhesive. If my parents found out, they'd freak. My quote-unquote *hobby* doesn't exactly jibe with the family brand. You can touch them if you want."

Whisper extended a shaky index finger and poked one mannequin's decomposing ribs. "Gross!" she cried, in the way most girls might say, *Awesome!*

"I can't believe you didn't run," Zuzu gushed. "You're, like, the fastest girl in school. I thought you'd be the first one out of here."

"I wanted to. But I was too scared." Whisper laughed once before releasing a bubbling stream of laughter.

Zuzu began laughing, too, but she wasn't sure why. Nothing Whisper said had been particularly funny. But the release felt good.

Suddenly Frannie called, "What's happening? Are those laughs of terror?"

"Laughs of terror?" Zuzu echoed. "That's not a thing."

This made Whisper and Zuzu laugh even harder.

"You can come back," Whisper called. "It wasn't Silas Hoke! It was just Zu—"

Zuzu slapped her hand over Whisper's mouth. "No one can know I'm here."

"Hmmm hmm-hmm mm-hmmmm?"

Zuzu removed her hand. "What?"

"Not even my friends?"

"You guys are fine. As long as you don't—"

"Zuzu?" Gemma said as she emerged from the fog. Frannie and Sophie trudged behind her like zombies.

"Hey." Zuzu waved awkwardly. She wasn't the cool "it girl" at school right now. She was a lone freak in a cemetery who'd just scared the wind out of four girls she barely knew.

"What's happening?" Gemma asked Whisper. She cut a look to the mannequins. "Are you okay?"

"Um, yeah, considering you guys took off and left me in a graveyard."

"We would never leave you," Frannie corrected. "We just hid. By the iron gates. On the other side."

"I'm sixty-five percent positive I puked all over beloved wife Betty Goldfarb," Sophie said.

"Don't worry. She's used to it," Zuzu explained. "Betty was a nurse."

"You knew her?" Whisper asked.

Zuzu was about to answer when Gemma said, "Are Paisley and Miranda hiding in the bushes or something?"

"No. They don't know I'm here. I came alone."

"You came to a cemetery *alone*?" Sophie asked.

Zuzu nodded. "It's my favorite—" She stopped herself. Not yet. "I wasn't completely alone." Then, to shake off their confused expressions, "I followed you."

"Ha!" Whisper pointed at her friends. "In your face! Not a crab!"

"Whoa, whoa, whoa," Gemma said. "Have you been spying on us?"

Zuzu took a deep breath. She had rehearsed her confession dozens of times but suddenly forgot everything she was going to say. "Spying? No. It was more of a curiosity thing. That turned into eavesdropping. That evolved into pursuing. That ended in following."

"Huh?" Sophie said for them all.

"I've seen you gathering at Paisley's house a few times and—"

"You mean *my* house?" Whisper snipped.

"Yes, your house, sorry," Zuzu said, her flesh burning with embarrassment. "You had on those cloaks and that black makeup. I asked Paisley what you were doing, but she made some stupid poop joke and went back to texting. So . . ."

"So *what?*" Gemma asked. "You spied on us?"

"It wasn't spying," Zuzu insisted. "I just happened to go to the bathroom while you were in Whisper's—"

"You eavesdropped?" Frannie asked.

"More like overheard." Zuzu shrugged. "Whisper's a loud talker."

The Grim Sleepers exchanged a terrified look.

"Don't worry, I won't tell anyone about your club."

"What do you want, Zuzu?" Gemma asked, cutting to the chase.

Another zing shot up Zuzu's spine. This one was fear. What if they rejected her? What if they told Miranda and Paisley about her dark side? What if they reenacted the prom scene from that old horror movie *Carrie* and doused her in pig's blood?

But what if they didn't?

"I want to join the Grim Sleepers," Zuzu managed.

"You?" Whisper said, loud enough to rattle the corpses. "But you're so . . ." She trailed off, but Zuzu knew exactly what was coming. She'd heard it a million times. "Cool."

There it was.

Sure, Zuzu looked cool. It was hard not to when you were styled by two of the most influential designers on the West Coast. But Zuzu didn't feel cool. She felt numb.

"You're even cooler," she said, meaning it.

They all laughed, assuming Zuzu was joking. She was not.

"I'm serious! Cool people just do their own thing and don't care what other people say. Like you guys. That's what makes you cool." *And that's what makes me uncool,* Zuzu didn't say. Admitting she was worried about what other people thought of her was too much truth for one night.

"What do you know about horror?" Sophie asked.

"Everything."

"How long have you liked it?" Frannie asked.

"Forever."

"How often do you think about it?" Whisper asked.

"Always."

"Prove it," Gemma said.

Zuzu hurried to fetch her bag from behind a tombstone.

"Is that real snakeskin?" Whisper asked.

"Yes," Zuzu bragged. "Limited edition."

Whisper looked more horrified than she had all night. "Yeah, no. We don't do animal skins of any kind."

"Uh, okay," Zuzu said, respecting Whisper even more.

"I think you should sell it and donate the money to PETA. And tell your parents to stop killing animals for fashion."

"I will," Zuzu promised as she pulled out her black hardcover journal.

"What is that?" Frannie asked, aiming her flashlight.

"Proof," Zuzu said. She opened her mouth to explain more but hesitated. Her parents and friends thought her notebooks held sketches of upcoming collections and outfit inspirations. If she showed these girls what they really contained, another piece of herself would be revealed. *What if they don't like it?*

What if they do?

Zuzu exhaled sharply. "I want to be a horror writer."

"What does that have to do with spying on us?" Gemma demanded.

"I practice by writing in the voices of monsters and madmen. Lately I've been channeling Silas Hoke."

Gemma perked up. "Like, really channeling? Are you a medium? Is he speaking through you?"

Zuzu shook her head. "I wish. But if he did, I think he'd say this . . ." With a trembling hand, she opened the journal to her Silas entries and handed it to Gemma. "Go ahead. Read it."

"*I've had my eye on these girls for a while now,*" Gemma began. "*Sixth graders. Best friends. Consumed with their dramatic little lives.*" She looked up from the page. "Wait, we're not 'consumed with our dramatic little lives.'"

"Speak for yourself," Frannie said.

Gemma smiled and continued: "*I know their names: Whisper, Frannie, Sophie, and Gemma. I know who their families are. I know where they live. How did I learn all this?*

"*How do you think?*

"*Killers come in all shapes and sizes, but most have one skill in common.*

"*The ability to creep up on you.*"

"Ew! Stop!" Whisper insisted. "It's kind of freaking me out."

Zuzu's heart sped up. "In a good way?"

"In a *great* way. You're a sick writer."

"It's not so hard when you've got a muse as sick as Silas," Sophie said.

Zuzu's insides warmed. The Grim Sleepers weren't running away or mocking her. They weren't posting her picture—they didn't even have their phones out. They were supporting her. The real her. The Zuzu who had been hiding for years.

"Follow me," she said. "Let me introduce you to some of my friends. Not Paisley and Miranda, I promise."

Zuzu took the lantern and strode confidently between grave markers as if walking the catwalk for a Jōhin fashion show. It was the first time Zuzu Otsuka was on the outside wanting in, but she certainly wasn't going to walk like it.

She stopped in front of a moss-coated obelisk. "This is my friend Helen Fulwig. She was trampled by a horse in 1902. Grew up in the South and hated winters in Misery Falls. On cold nights, you can see her warm breath rising up from the earth."

"That's not true," Frannie begged. "Is it?"

"I believe it is," Zuzu said.

"Me too!" Gemma said, finally letting down her guard. "The supernatural is real."

Zuzu indicated a flat stone in tangled weeds. Carved into the rock were a skull and crossbones, except the crossbones were made to look like baseball bats.

"This is my buddy Boris Leadbetter. Professional base-ball player. Took a nasty inside fastball to the head in 1983. Sometimes when you put your ear to Boris's grave, you can hear a crowd chanting his name."

"How do you know their stories?" Gemma asked.

"I dug up their obituaries at the library."

Zuzu stopped before one of the tallest monuments in the graveyard: a ten-foot statue of an angel cradling a sleeping girl.

Sophie gulped. "Is that—"

All four friends looked down at the words carved into the base.

GINNY BAKER
BELOVED DAUGHTER. DEAR FRIEND.
DEDICATED STUDENT.

TAKEN TOO SOON

"On nights like tonight, when the fog is thick . . ."

Frannie covered her ears. "Don't say it, don't say it, don't say it—"

"You can see the ghostly shape of a one-legged girl hobbling around the cemetery."

Frannie groaned.

"Have your living friends ever met your dead friends?" Sophie asked. She didn't miss a thing.

"Uh, no." Zuzu leaned against Ginny Baker's stone angel. "Understatement alert: they would not get along."

"Why are you even friends with them?" Whisper asked. Voice aside, the girl was not afraid to speak up.

"We're into a lot of the same things. You know, like fashion and influencers and . . . I don't know. We have a bunch of inside jokes and stuff."

"But they don't like horror?" Gemma asked.

"One time I turned on the movie *Ginger Snaps*. They didn't even make it to the part when Ginger snaps. It's not their thing, so I just keep it to myself, you know?"

The four girls looked at her blankly.

"They're not as bad as you think."

The girls didn't look convinced, which was fine. Zuzu wasn't there to sell them on Miranda and Paisley—only herself. "So, about me joining the Grim Sleepers."

"You really want in?" Gemma asked.

"I think the anonymous text and the leaping corpses speak for themselves."

"You may not feel the same after hearing one of Whisper's stories," Frannie cracked.

Zuzu dared a smile. "I already heard one, remember? 'Vincent the Vaccinated Vampire.'"

Whisper pulled her beanie over her face.

"You just need to tap into your dark side," Zuzu told her. "Do that and you'll have us all screaming like Sally Hardesty."

"Is she buried here, too?" Sophie asked.

Zuzu gasped. "Sally Hardesty? *The Texas Chain Saw Massacre*? Anyone?"

The girls made faces, trying to place the title. They had a lot to learn.

Zuzu couldn't wait to teach them.

"I did have a darker idea once," Whisper peeped. "But it's pretty gross."

"Yes!" Zuzu said. "Tell it over there, by Obert Starr's grave. Obert got caught between the cars of an old-fashioned roller coaster and ended up smeared all along the rails. It doesn't get much grosser than that."

Zuzu led them over, the growl of the nearby creek growing louder. It was a decent grave by Crimson Creek Cemetery standards. Obert must've still had relatives to occasionally prune the overgrowth. Zuzu sat down so she was roughly six feet above Obert's head, placed the lantern in front of her, and gestured for the others to sit.

Whisper sat last. "I don't know, you guys. We don't have our cloaks or the Chalice of Cherubs or—"

"We're in a graveyard," Zuzu said, "at night. What else do you need?"

Whisper glanced at her friends. They encouraged her with thumbs-ups and *go ahead* nods. "All right." She exhaled. "Consider yourselves warned."

Gemma gave Zuzu a side-eyed look. "Did you happen to learn our incantation while you were spying?"

"I wasn't spying!" Zuzu insisted. "But yes. Yes, I did."

Frannie turned off her flashlight, and they began.

> *"Come, ghost,*
> *Come, monster,*
> *Come, devilkin,*
> *Tonight's story is about to begin."*

Three times they said it, their voices weaving around the crumbling gravestones. Zuzu imagined her dead friends clawing out of their graves just enough to hear the story.

Whisper closed her eyes, as if sinking into the darkness she'd been denying herself for so long. Then, in a voice stronger and clearer than any of them had ever heard, she began.

"Tonight, I will tell a tale called '1-2-3-4, I Declare a Thumb War.'"

A WARNING
TO THE READER

If you want to hear this story, you must hear
it the way we do. From start to finish.

You are not allowed to get a snack. You cannot
use the bathroom. You cannot text your friends.
You cannot stop halfway. You must be brave.
You must stay strong.

You must survive until the very end.

1-2-3-4,
I DECLARE A THUMB WAR

PART
one

Click, clack, tick, tap.

Even in her dreams, Agnes hears it: the clacking of fingernails tapping against her phone. Forget the sounds of ocean waves or singing birds. Nothing beats the sound of a fast, crisp text. How dreamy.

Before her eyes are even open, Agnes's thumbs are eager to start the day. They press the thumbprint sensor, swipe open her apps, and start scrolling while Agnes is still widening her sleepy eyes. The glow of fresh messages is better than sunshine.

> **OMG did u see Sara's IG post?**

Jilly's text wakes her like a cold shower. Agnes's thumbs scurry across the keypad before her brain knows what they're doing.

> **Right? R those short bangs or tall eyebrows?**

Forget breakfast. Forget today's frog-dissection assignment. Forget climate change, pandemics, and war. In Agnes's world, Sara's bangs are the number one trending topic.

"Agnes!" her mom shouts from the kitchen. "Stop with the clickety-clack and get ready for school!"

Inside the shower, a wire caddy dangles from the faucet handle. It's supposed to hold Agnes's shampoo, body scrub, and loofahs. But she uses it to hold her phone.

When she brushes her teeth, her phone is propped up on the mouthwash. When she gets dressed, it's on a pile of laundry. When she puts on her shoes, it's wedged between her knees. The girl is ob*sessed.*

In the kitchen, Agnes's cold breakfast sits on a plate. Her mom has already finished eating and is putting on her white doctor's coat.

"Sorry I'm late," Agnes mumbles.

"This is the one time all day I get to see you," her mom says. "Five minutes with my only kid. Is that too much to ask?"

Agnes drops into her chair and says, "It's not my fault. Jilly had an emergency."

"Sounded like it," her mom says. *"Click, clack, tick, tap."* Then she tosses a glossy pamphlet on the table. On the cover is a bunch of smiling kids sitting on a grassy campus lawn, looking freakishly happy. And the creepiest part is that none of them have phones.

Agnes reads the title.

JAMESON TECH-TOX CAMP FOR JUVENILES

"Ew!" Agnes drops the pamphlet like it's burst into flames. "What is a tech-tox?"

"Technology detox," her mom says. "It seems like a nice place, Agnes. They treat tech addictions and—"

"Mom! I am not some kind of addict!"

"Agnes! Look at your thumbs! You're texting right now!"

Agnes looks down. Without realizing it, she's already texting Jilly, Olive, and Petra:

Dyinnnng!! You will NOT believe what
my mom just gave me.

"Enough!" her mother yells. She grabs the phone from
Agnes's hands and slams it down on the far end of the
table. "Don't you remember when you were little? How
happy you were just going on walks with me? Petting the
neighborhood dogs? Listening to the birds sing?"

"Sorry I'm not a toddler anymore," Agnes says.

"You were *present*, that's all I'm saying." Then her mother gasps. "Agnes, your fingers! What is *wrong* with you?"

Agnes looks down to find her hand crawling toward the phone like a gigantic spider. She bolts up from the table and grabs her phone. "Nothing is *wrong* with me, Mom. I just need someone to talk to, and you're always working."

"That's because I'm in *surgery*, Agnes. I'm saving people's lives. What are *you* doing with your time?"

💀

"Jameson Tech-Tox Camp for Juveniles," Agnes mutters as she stomps down the sidewalk. "Jameson Lose-Contact-With-All-Your-Friends Camp is more like it. And *Juveniles*? Really? Where is this camp? 1952?"

Agnes checks her phone. Then she rubs her eyes and checks again.

Because, really? Somehow in the last ten minutes she's responded to six texts, posted two pics, and sent a streak of chats on her socials. And she doesn't remember doing any of it.

Then she dares to think the unthinkable.

What if she *does* have a problem?

Maybe it wouldn't hurt to take a teeny tiny tech-tox, she thinks. Just to prove she can. Agnes unzips a pocket of her backpack, slides in her phone, and hoists the bag onto her back, out of reach.

Agnes looks around the neighborhood and smiles. Look—dogs! Listen—birds! Then—*Ka-sss!*

Did someone just take a picture? She gazes around. There's nobody. Then she notices the weight in her palm: 5.78 ounces, to be exact.

Her backpack is dangling from one shoulder again, and the phone is back in her hands. Sure enough, there's a picture of a bird on the screen. And she's already posting it.

When the heck did that happen?

Agnes can find her school locker blindfolded. All she has to do is follow the sound of tapping thumbnails.

Click, clack, tick, tap, click, clack, tick, tap . . .

As usual, her best friends, aka the Clawz, are leaning against their lockers, their manicured fingers hard at work.

"Hey, guys," Agnes says.

"Hey," they mumble back. Not one looks up from her phone.

Are they—as Mom put it—*addicted*? Agnes deletes the stupid thought. It's not like they have to look at her face when they speak to her. They know what it looks like! It's all over her socials.

"I've had a brutal morning," Agnes says. "My mom—"

"We read," Jilly interrupts. "What a joke."

"She means well," Agnes says. "She just—"

"Agnes, where are you on my story?" Petra demands. "My outfit of the day isn't going to like itself."

Agnes finds Petra's story. There. Liked.

Then Jilly says, "Ag. You're fading."

Yes, Jilly is actually looking at Agnes. Well, at her fingernails, anyway. They are long, filed into points, and painted with pink Pansy-Pants polish. But yeah, the white *A-G-N-E-S* letters aren't as bold as they were a few days earlier.

You see, there are four girls in the Clawz. Each girl has five letters in her name and five fingers on her right hand. So *J-I-L-L-Y* is spelled out in tiger-striped letters on Jilly's fingernails: *J* on the thumb, *I* on the index finger, and so on. Olive has *O-L-I-V-E* in cobwebby print, and Petra has *P-E-T-R-A* spelled out in neon colors.

"I'll refresh them in math," Agnes says.

Jilly looks at Agnes suspiciously. "It's like you've totally stopped caring."

Olive's squeal saves the day.

"Eee! Jason's texting back. Ugh, he's got the slowest thumbs ever. These three little dots are *killing* me."

1-2-3-4,
I DECLARE A THUMB WAR

PART
two

When the first-period bell rings, Agnes heads to Biology. Everything is going fine until—*Skwert!* Something red splashes all over Agnes's face. It's warm and gooey and smells like pennies.

Blood!

"Ack! Get it off! Get it off!"

She's about to puke and pass out simultaneously when she feels a paper towel swiping her eyes, her nose, her cheeks.

"All gone," Mr. Scaletti says. "You can stop screaming now."

Agnes shuts her mouth and cracks open an eye. The entire Biology class is staring at her. So are their dead dissected frogs.

Then someone whispers, "Are you okay?"

It's Adrian, her lab partner. Messy blond hair. Wrinkled T-shirt. Palms scuffed and scraped, like he uses his hands to do stuff outdoors. Agnes hates being outdoors. It's so hard to read messages in direct sunlight.

"Looks like you snipped the femoral artery."

"Sorry," she tells him. "My scalpel was over by the pancreas and my thumb jerked—"

She cuts herself off. Her thumbs again. It's like they have minds of their own.

"It happens," he says.

"How would you know?"

"I've been dissecting frogs since I was a kid."

Agnes takes a step back. "So . . . what? You're, like, a frog assassin?"

Adrian scoffs. "No! I'd find dead ones by my grandfather's pond and . . . whatever. It doesn't matter. I'm into science, that's all." Then he removes a battered old pocketknife from his jeans and unfolds it.

"Dude!" Agnes instinctively curls her hands into fists to protect her precious texting thumbs. "What are you *doing*?"

Adrian says, "Sorry. I only dissect with my Buck knife. The blade is sharper."

"If Mr. Scaletti sees that, you're dead."

"Better not let him see it, then." Adrian slips the handle up his sleeve and starts cutting. The confident way he pushes those frog intestines aside is kind of . . . hot?

Agnes never paid Adrian much attention before. He lives in her neighborhood, and they ride the same bus, but he always sits alone and stares out the window. No devices, no anything.

"Do you even have a phone?" Agnes asks.

Adrian looks up at her, his knife dripping blood. "That's a random question."

Agnes gasps when she sees his eyes. *Have they always been that green?*

"But no," he says, "I don't. Never saw the point."

"Cool," Agnes says, even though it's not. She could never date a guy without socials. How would flirting even work?

Later that night, Agnes is home alone, microwaving dinner. What else is she going to do? Her mom is working late. Again. Saving more lives.

Then, mid-chat, Agnes's phone battery dies. She quickly plugs it in and says to her empty kitchen, "See, Mom? I can save lives, too."

While she's waiting for it to charge, Agnes notices the tech-tox pamphlet on the counter and thinks about her mother. She's been so worried lately, and that makes Agnes sad. Her mother is all she has. If anything happens to her . . .

Agnes picks up the pamphlet to kill time. Then—*Ding.* Her dinner is ready. But it can wait. She starts reading and—*Ping.* Her phone is alive!

Agnes's thumbs jerk, desperate to check her notifications. But her eight fingers hold tight, and she forces her thumbs to help unfold the pamphlet. She's determined to read it.

It doesn't go well.

Her left thumb pierces the photo of a reflecting pool. Then her right thumb slashes a model's face.

The whole thing is starting to scare her. But what is she going to do, google solutions on her phone? Her phone is the problem. No, that's wrong. Her *thumbs* are the problem. They must be stopped.

Agnes charges into the garage in her pajamas and bare feet. She grabs black duct tape and glares at her thumbs.

"I don't want to do this," she says. "You two are forcing me."

Her thumbs bend down like scolded dogs.

"Don't give me that look," she says. "Wait. What am I even saying?"

Agnes unspools some tape and, with the help of her teeth, binds her thumbs to her hands. There: problem solved. The tape will ruin the fresh coat of Pansy-Pants polish she put on during math class, but that's the least of her troubles.

She returns to her bed and plugs in her phone—way on the other side of the room. She goes under the covers and tries to finish reading the battered tech-tox pamphlet. She stares at the group of friends on that lawn, all of whom are incredibly *present*, and wonders what that must be like.

Snick. The fall of an autumn leaf.

Grack. The morning call of a hungry robin.

Plick. A drop of morning dew from the tree outside the window.

Snap. Twigs breaking beneath the feet of early morning walkers.

Agnes smiles in her sleep.

Then—*Click, clack, tick, tap.*

Her eyes shoot open. She's no longer in bed. She's on the floor. Way on the other side of the room, where her phone is plugged in. There's a trail of shredded black tape behind her, and her thumbs are speeding across the phone's keypad.

"Stop!" she yells.

Her thumbs ignore her. They're texting so fast, she can't keep up. Agnes leans over and scrolls up with her nose to read her thumbs' recent texts.

To Petra:

> Idea for your outfit of the day: put a bag over your head. You'll get tons of likes. 🧛

To Jilly:

> Don't worry about my nails. Worry about your eyebrows (and your thighs and your breath). 🐛 🐷 🤢

To Olive:

> FYI Jason is going to dump you. I found out he's allergic to dogs. 🤧 🐶 🚮

Those aren't even the worst of it. Choking with horror, Agnes watches as a series of the most unflattering selfies she's ever taken, including the one of her in her bathrobe with an unflushed toilet behind her—the selfies she *trashed* but didn't *delete* from her trash—get sent to *every single contact in her phone.*

"No! Stop!" she screams.

To Agnes's surprise, the thumbs do stop. They go rigid, dropping the phone. Then both thumbs point left. Agnes looks.

Slashed across the wall in smeared thumbprints the color of jolly pink Pansy-Pants is a dripping message.

1-2-3-4,
I DECLARE A THUMB WAR

PART
three

Agnes's mom is nowhere to be found. From the looks of it, she never came home last night. Agnes gives her phone a wary look before picking it up and dialing.

Her mom picks up on the first ring.

"Agnes." Her voice is breathless. "I'm sorry I didn't call. There's a—a situation. I've been stuck at the hospital all night."

"A situation?"

"I can't talk now."

"Mom, what's going on?"

Agnes hears a scream.

"Stay home from school today, okay? I have to go."

"But, Mom—I need to tell you about—"

"You hear me? Don't leave the house. I'll call when I can."

The signal goes dead. She's gone.

Agnes stares at her phone in shock.

Going to school is the last thing Agnes wants to do. Those terrible texts she sent. That her *thumbs* sent. The selfies. The endless humiliating selfies. But she needs to smooth things over with the Clawz, and she can't do that on the phone. Who knows what her thumbs will do next?

💀

At school, Jilly, Olive, and Petra stare straight at Agnes as she walks toward them. They're not even on their phones. It's *that* bad.

"Oh, I see," Jilly seethes. "Your mom let *you* keep your phone."

Agnes looks down. She's passing it between her hands. She had no idea.

"Where are your phones?" she asks. Now everyone in school is looking at her. Not a single person has a device. "I don't understand."

The crowd closes in.

"Will someone tell me what's going on?" she cries.

Her panic is enough to make Petra believe her. But it's not enough to get her off the hook.

"Um, that email you wrote to Principal Murphy last night?" Petra asks.

"What email?"

"The one where you said you were getting cyber-bullied by every single person in school?"

"I didn't say that," Agnes tells her.

"Stop trying to act all innocent. He forwarded it to all of our parents. They confiscated our phones, Agnes."

Agnes is surprisingly relieved. Maybe they didn't see her texts. But then Jilly says, "But not before we got your texts. Funny, how our parents think *we* were bullying *you*." Her eyes get all teary. "How could you say those things?"

"Seriously, Agnes," Olive adds. "Why?"

Cold sweat rolls down Agnes's back. How can she tell them what's been going on? They'll never believe her. Besides, it's too late. The entire student body is flexing their fingers and moving toward her.

Agnes looks closer.

No—not their fingers.

They're flexing their *thumbs*. Massaging them. Like they ache. Agnes shudders. She knows exactly what they're feeling.

She also knows what will happen if those thumbs don't get what they want.

Agnes turns and runs.

At home, Agnes locks the doors and calls her mom. And calls. And calls. The first several times, Mom picks up—but each time, Agnes's thumbs kill the call before they can talk.

Pretty soon, her mom stops answering. Agnes can't blame her. And yet she does. She needs her mother. Who knows what her thumbs will do next?

Will they find scissors and chop off her hair?

Or will they find other uses for sharp objects?

Cut off her tongue?

Stab her eyes?

Agnes throws her phone aside and gets into bed. She can't take it anymore. Her thumbs are itchy and twitchy. She stares at her ceiling for hours, contemplating the remainder of her lonely, terrifying, sleepless life.

Then she hears it.

Tap. Tap. Tap.

Agnes tells herself it could be lots of things. Wood can pop and crack inside old houses. Sometimes the bathroom faucets drip.

Though this sounds like it's coming from the front door.

What if the Clawz have come to cut her throat?

"Go away," Agnes whines. "Pleeeease."

Tap. Tap. Tap.

A worse thought occurs: What if it's Mom, injured and unable to open the door? What if Agnes finds her dead out there tomorrow, the front door rubbed raw from her dying taps?

Tap. Tap. Tap.

Agnes takes a trembling breath.

She sits up.

And places her bare feet on the cold floor.

💀

The sounds are louder in the living room.

TAP. TAP. TAP.

She peers through a window. She doesn't see her mom. She doesn't see the Clawz.

TAP-TAP-TAP-TAP-TAP-TAP-TAP-TAP-TAP.

Agnes wraps her hand around the icy knob.

"Hello? Who's there?"

The noises accelerate. Soft. Fleshy. Urgent.

TAP-TAP-TAP-TAP-TAP-TAP-TAP-TAP-TAP—

She opens the door.

Cold night air gusts in. For a moment, Agnes thinks it snowed. That's why it's so cold. That's why her front lawn is blanketed in—

No. That's not snow.

Those are thumbs.

Thousands of severed thumbs.

All pointing at Agnes.

1-2-3-4,
I DECLARE A THUMB WAR

PART
four

Agnes tries to slam the door.

Instead of the *thump* of wood, there's a rubbery bounce. The door strikes a half dozen thumbs trying to wriggle inside.

"Skreeeee!!!"

It's the panicky high-pitched sound of pigs being led to slaughter.

Agnes stumbles backward into the house. The door bursts open. She stares in shock as squished, damaged thumbs with broken nails and blood blisters wobble around dizzily—before facing Agnes again.

The entire yard ripples as the severed thumbs begin to hop forward.

Agnes runs from the thundering *TAP-TAP-TAP-TAP* of thumbs clambering into her house. Agnes screams, and screams again, and screams some more as she backs into her room. Her foot clips the side of the door—

And she falls. Whimpering, she kicks her feet out to close the bedroom door, but it's too late. A wave of thumbs splashes into the room. They crawl up her legs and scurry along her body. A thumb lands on her forehead and bends over to point at Agnes's eyes.

Its nail is painted with a tiger-striped *J*.

Jilly's thumb.

It is joined by a thumb at either side, one's nail painted *O*, the other *P*.

Olive. Petra.

"No!" Agnes cries. "What have you done to my friends?!"

The *J* thumb curls its knuckles as if to leap. Into Agnes's gaping mouth? Is that their plan? To choke her?

Then the *J* thumb straightens.

It quivers, as though sniffing the air like a dog.

The *O* thumb and the *P* thumb do the same. All the thumbs on Agnes's body start quivering too.

Her phone. It's on her bedside table.

The thumbs smell it. Sense it. Whatever—They *want* it. What happened to Jilly, Olive, Petra, and the rest of the kids at school happened because their thumbs didn't have access to their phones. The thumbs are desperate for a hit. Agnes's mother was right. They're addicted.

The thumbs hop across Agnes's face like a stampede of mice. Agnes feels the squishy severed ends plop over her eyelids. Jagged thumbnails scuttle through her hair like beetles. Blood smears across her lips.

Agnes fights her way up from the floor, tossing off a dozen thumbs.

She lurches for the bedroom door.

But a second wave of thumbs rounds the corner.

Agnes pulls a one-eighty and scurries around her bed. Thumbs pop and crack beneath her bare feet, *skree*-ing in pain, spasming like stomped cockroaches.

She zeroes in on the window—she's got to get outside! That means planting her foot next to her phone, which is swarming with a wiggling hill of thumbs.

With a mighty swipe of her arm, Agnes sends the thumbs flying. Quickly she steps on the cleared table, opens her window, and punches out the screen. Right before crawling through, she takes one last look at her screen.

The *J*, *O*, and *P* thumbs have reached the phone. And they're sending an endless stream of texts to other thumbs.

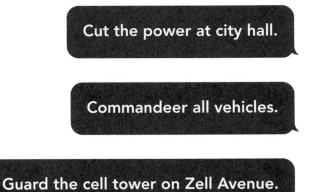

Cut the power at city hall.

Commandeer all vehicles.

Guard the cell tower on Zell Avenue.

Agnes jumps.

She lands on the ground beside her house. There are screams. Some near, some distant. Girls, boys, men, women.

Agnes darts into her front yard and stops cold. Thumbs. Everywhere. As far as the eye can see.

Thousands of thumbs stampede like rats across roads, sidewalks, driveways, and lawns. They take turns hopping down chimneys. They trail up the sides of houses. Catapult through open windows.

In a daze, Agnes plods toward the street.

"This can't be happening."

A car barrels by, obliterating trash cans left and right. Agnes catches a terrifying glimpse of the teenage driver. His hands on the steering wheel have bleeding stumps were his thumbs used to be. But there are plenty of *other* thumbs. They waggle from inside his mouth, nostrils, ears, eyes.

"This can't be happening!"

People run shrieking through the neighborhood, looking like they're on fire. But those aren't flames. They are thumbs hooked tightly to clothing. Nightgowns bulge as the thumbs dig out innards.

"THIS CAN'T BE HAPPENING!"

A sudden sharp pain hits Agnes in the shin. She cries out as her back slams onto the sidewalk. A skateboard has run into her. Two rows of severed thumbs are propelling it like they're rowing a boat.

The thumbs hop off the skateboard and onto Agnes.

She tightens her arms around her face and screams. She knows it won't do any good. The thumbs will writhe past her elbows, slither inside her mouth, wiggle down her throat, push into her eye sockets.

Then—*Whoosh!*

"*Skree!*"

Whoosh!

"*Skree!*"

She opens one eye. Thumbs are flying, being cut in two, screaming.

Adrian is standing above her, slicing and dicing, his Buck knife coated in blood.

☠

Adrian helps Agnes onto the skateboard.

"Is this yours?"

"No!"

"Do you know how to control this thing?"

He doesn't answer, because what other choice do they have?

Agnes wraps her arms around Adrian's waist as he begins to propel the board. With a throaty rumble, the

skateboard speeds up. Luckily, thumbs hurl themselves out of the way.

Except for the slow ones. They get run over and squirt thumb guts.

Power boxes are exploding atop electrical poles. Streetlights go dark. Zooming over the neighborhood are drones carrying thumb riders—and, below, the remote controls are being operated by thumb pilots. People try to take cover in cars, homes, garages, but the thumbs seem to have rewired the security systems.

No one can escape.

Adrian hops off the skateboard, grabs Agnes's hand, and runs toward a grove of dark trees.

"Wait! Why would we want to go into the woods right now?"

"No people means no thumbs!"

He's right. Nothing but nature. They plunge into the undergrowth and dodge slashing branches for several minutes.

"Can't we stop?" Agnes begs. "Catch our breath?"

They collapse in the clear blue moonlight, panting and sweating. Agnes rolls onto her stomach and sobs.

And feels something squirm up her spine.

She springs to a sitting position.

"Get it off get it off get it off!"

Adrian reaches into her hair and tugs. Agnes feels the twist of a severed thumb unwilling to let go. Adrian gives another pull, and Agnes feels a clump of her hair get yanked out.

No time for pain. Agnes turns and finds Adrian has the thumb pinned to the grass. Agnes shrieks when she sees its nail: a tiger-striped *J*.

"Kill it!" she begs.

The tip of Adrian's blade sinks into the thumb tip with a juicy *squish*. As efficiently as with the frog in Biology class, he removes a layer of flesh.

Packed inside the thumb is a tiny yellow brain.

It squirms with a light sucking sound.

"How is this happening?" Agnes pleads.

Adrian sighs. "Phones emit low-grade radiation. When people's thumbs are pressed against their phones all day, they must get enough radiation to cause mutations. In time, the severed thumbs will probably grow eyes, ears, even limbs. Eventually they will outnumber us two to one. And we won't be very good at fighting because—"

"Because we won't have thumbs," Agnes guesses. "But you will."

Adrian nods. He doesn't need to say anything else. Agnes knows the rest.

Soon mutant thumbs will infiltrate every electrical system, punishing humans for relying too much on technology—for not being *present*. Traffic lights will go on the fritz. Subway cars will get trapped inside tunnels. Hydroelectric dams will fail. Airplanes will fall out of the sky. Only cellular phone towers will remain, so the thumbs can communicate. And their rallying cry will be *click, clack, tip, tap.*

Agnes feels a peculiar sensation. An aching. A pinching. Even a ripping.

She lifts her hands into the moonlight.

Her thumbs have dislocated from their sockets and are wiggling wildly. Ribbons of skin are all that keep them attached to her hands.

The fact that Agnes feels no pain only makes it more horrifying.

She thinks of her mom and the crisis at the hospital. This was the crisis. People's thumbs must be revolting all over the country. Maybe all over the world.

"I'm sorry, Agnes," Adrian says, "but it'll be faster if I do it."

Agnes takes a shivering inhale.

"I know."

She holds out her hands. Her thumbs spin madly. Beneath each thumbprint, Agnes sees the pulsing of a mutant brain.

Adrian holds her wrists firmly.

"Skreeee! Skreeee!"

He holds the blade of his knife to the base of one thumb.

"There's going to be blood. I'd look away if I were you."

But Agnes is already half gone, eyes closed, dreaming of the Jameson Tech-Tox Camp for Juveniles campus. It's a beautiful spring day. The sky is sapphire blue. The breeze is soft and smells like honeysuckle. Smiling friends wave her over to the quad. Adrian is there. He challenges her to a thumb war. She accepts. He lets her win, just like he always does. He winks and reaches for her hand. She gives it to him.

They hold on tight.

"*SKREEEEEEEEE!!!*"

Zuzu didn't know Whisper could *skreeeeeee* that loud until she did. Zuzu didn't know *anyone* could. The girls screamed like five emergency sirens going off at once.

And Whisper's devious dark side, with some encouragement from Zuzu, had ignited it all.

"How did you do that?" Sophie asked. "It was next-level!"

"I dug deep," Whisper said, her proud smile aimed at Zuzu.

Zuzu smiled back, happy to help. Also happy to stay on Whisper's good side. It was clear who'd inspired that story, and Zuzu wanted it known that, while she was friends with Paisley and Miranda, she was *not* Paisley and Miranda.

"We have a new Scream Scale record," Gemma announced. "An eight!"

Whisper *skreeeeee*ed again, clutched her head, and rolled onto her back, not seeming to care that Obert Starr was just six feet below her. "I don't believe it!"

"*I* believe it," Zuzu said. "There haven't been this many screams in Crimson Creek Cemetery since the night they found Silas Hoke nailing Ginny Baker's leg to himself."

The second Zuzu said it, the dark night got darker.

Thonk.

For a moment, they all pretended they hadn't heard it.

"Zuzu," Whisper said, "please tell me that's you."

Zuzu shook her head. At least, she wanted to. It suddenly felt too heavy to move. "My *thonk*ing boards are way over there."

Thonk-thonk.

"Then what's that?" Frannie demanded.

"Don't ask *me*," Zuzu replied. "Unless we screamed loud enough to—"

"Wake the dead," Gemma finished.

THONK-THONK!

Zuzu didn't know who ran first. She also didn't know the last time she'd felt pure terror from a real-life situation. Or the last time she'd choked on her gum. It was horrifying. It was nauseating. It was incredible.

As the five girls ran up Moss Street with Whisper's fleet feet leading the charge, Zuzu's biggest fear wasn't getting mauled by the ghost of Silas Hoke. It was that Paisley and Miranda would find out about her secret and mess it all up.

FRANNIE

Frannie stopped outside the double doors of the Misery Falls Middle School theater. Her lungs were like clenched fists. When she tried to take hold of the door handle, her sweaty palm slipped right off.

This was no way for the star of the show to feel on the first afternoon of rehearsals.

Anyone without extracurriculars had put on their swim gear and gone straight from school to the waterfalls that gave Misery Falls its name, to participate in the freezing-cold Hoke Soak: a brash show of courage against Silas Hoke's fear of water.

So Frannie was alone.

Without the usual hallway bustle, she noticed architectural details. She smelled floor polish, wood, and metal

165

instead of the overpowering funk of pit sweat, drugstore cologne, and sweet perfume. She could hear the distant slapping of a janitor's mop: *thwack-thwack*.

At least, Frannie hoped it was a janitor. She was still rattled from the night before. They all were. No one, including Gemma, had any explanation for it. Frannie had been checking her phone constantly, expecting a breaking news story about a missing girl or a report of open caskets at Crimson Creek Cemetery. But it was just a normal Wednesday. So much so that Frannie wondered if her dramatic mind had made the whole thing up.

Eager for a distraction, she shoved open both doors— with the strength of a leading lady, not some lowly Baby Can—and entered with a flourish. "Hellll-o!" she trilled.

The theater was dark. The stage curtains were drawn.

Frannie checked her phone: 3:58 p.m. Two minutes early. Where was everyone?

"Welcome," said a female voice.

"Ahh!" Frannie shouted.

DayNa was sitting in the front row of seats. In the dark. Wearing her usual all black.

"Did I get . . . ? Are we not . . . ?"

DayNa snapped Ms. Snowden's binder shut and stood. "Everyone else is starting tomorrow." She gestured at the stage. "I called you here for a *fuse*."

"Oh," Frannie said. "A fuse. Okay." She nodded sagely while her brain scrambled to define the term. She thought she knew every piece of theater terminology there was, from *emotional recall* to *fourth wall*. What the heck was a fuse? Or did DayNa simply mean a fuse had gone out, hence the darkness?

The double doors opened again.

Miranda. The understudy. That word gave Frannie a ticklish thrill followed by a punch of anxiety. Miranda would never let weeks of rehearsals go by without a fight.

For now, though, Miranda appeared to have given up. Her backpack was not fashionably hooked over one shoulder but worn with both straps buckled tight, like she was about to hike off into the woods forever. Anything was better than being Frannie Vargas-Stein's understudy.

Miranda gave the sleepy theater the same dumbfounded look Frannie had. "Are we conserving energy?"

"It's a *fuse*," Frannie said with authority she didn't have.

Miranda's eyebrows knitted together. Then—"Oh. A fuse. Great. Cool."

DayNa scampered up the side stairs of the stage and drew open the curtains. "Behold!"

Revealed was a long table stacked with papers.

"These scripts need to be collated and stapled," DayNa said.

167

"Copy machines can do that, you know," Miranda said.

"I'd rather you two do it."

"I'm an actor," Miranda huffed. "Not a stapler."

"*One who staples*," Frannie corrected. "A stapler is an inanimate object."

"Then *you* must be the stapler," Miranda retorted, "based on your acting."

And you must be the understudy, based on your *acting,* Frannie wanted to say, but she thought better of it.

"Good news, girls," DayNa said. "This afternoon, you're *both* staplers."

Frannie felt her skin heat up like the stage lights were on after all.

"This isn't fair," Miranda said. "Why just us?"

"Because this is a *fuse*," DayNa replied. Based off their blank expressions, she added, "You will both be playing Audrey, which means you need to become *one*. I need your performances to be interchangeable. Thus the two of you must fuse—or *bond* if you want to be passé about it."

Frannie stole a glance at Miranda, who was gaping in sheer horror.

"How will stapling papers fuse us?" Miranda demanded.

"You'll have to become one and work in harmony to get it done. And you must get it done. We can't start rehearsal tomorrow without scripts."

"This could take hours!" Frannie cried. Missing the Hoke Soak for rehearsal was one thing. Missing it to staple papers with Miranda was quite another.

"At least it's only one hundred and twelve pages," DayNa said. "The script for *Twelve Angry DayNas* was three times longer." She tossed a key chain, which Frannie caught against her chest. "Lock up when you're done."

"Wait—You're leaving?" Frannie hadn't been alone with Miranda since fifth grade.

"Fuse, Audreys! Fuse!"

And with that, DayNa was gone.

Frannie quickly turned back to the table, if only to hide her nervousness. What she wouldn't give for all those thumbs from Whisper's story! They could swarm the table, organize these stacks in minutes, and then, as a fun bonus, scuttle up Miranda's neck and wipe that *I just guzzled curdled milk* expression off her face.

"We need a system," Frannie said flatly. She was an actor. She could at least *act* professional. "How about I collate the first half, you do the second half, and then we'll put them together?"

"Why do you get the first half?" Miranda snipped. "Because you're the lead?"

"Fine, you take the first half," Frannie said. "I'll give my all to *any* part I play."

Miranda began sorting through the stacks of papers. "You give your all, all right. To stealing my role."

Frannie snatched a stack and began riffling through it. "I didn't steal it. DayNa—" She cut herself off, hoping to douse the smoldering anger that was building inside her. Best to finish the job and get out of there.

She directed her attention to the purrs of flipping papers, the bite of the stapler, their agitated sighs. Finally, a surprise note:

"Sssss!"

Frannie looked up to find Miranda grimacing and clutching her thumb. Whisper's story flashed back into Frannie's mind. Was it coming true? Were Miranda's thumbs starting to revolt?

"What happened?" Frannie asked.

"Paper cut," Miranda grunted. "Not your problem."

Frannie winced at the blood dripping down Miranda's wrist. It was kind of bad. But what was she supposed to do? Miranda was already digging a bandage out of her bag.

"Classic Frannie," she said. "Letting me bleed to death."

"'Classic Frannie'? More like classic Miranda."

"How is it classic me?"

"Uh, April Fools' Day? The *ta-ran-tu-la*?"

The four syllables reverberated across the empty stage. For two years, neither Frannie nor Miranda had mentioned it. Miranda was probably too ashamed. Frannie, meanwhile, was too proud. But the previous night at Crimson Creek Cemetery had changed that. Whisper had been brave enough to release her inner demons, and so would Frannie.

Miranda scoffed. "Oh please. You were doing an oral presentation on arachnids. I was only trying to help."

"Putting your brother's tarantula in my hood right before I took center stage is what you call *help*?"

Miranda slammed down her papers. "You were failing that class. You needed extra credit. And you know how much Mr. Sacco likes visual aids."

Frannie's face was on fire. "Your visual aid had nothing to do with helping me!"

"No? Then why would I do it?"

"Because you're a competitive social-climbing saboteur! Paisley was popular and you wanted to impress her! Miranda, she was our nemesis—and you turned on me!"

"'Saboteur'? 'Nemesis'?" Miranda rolled her eyes. "You're so dramatic."

"Well, it's pretty dramatic when you're standing in front of the class giving a presentation and a tarantula crawls across your cheek!"

"It was April Fools' Day. Take a joke, Frannie."

"*Make* a joke, Miranda. There was nothing funny about that day."

Frannie couldn't bring herself to say what had happened next. They both knew it, anyway. The whole school did. The second Frannie felt that hairy spider creep across her face, she'd peed her jeans. Her brand-new white jeans. In front of the entire class. For the rest of the year, everyone called her Tinkle Bell.

It hurt. But nothing was more painful than seeing Paisley high-five Miranda when Frannie ran from the classroom in tears.

"You humiliated your best friend so Paisley would like you."

Miranda crossed her arms and stared out at the double doors. "If that's how you want to remember it, fine."

"I don't *want* to remember it at all. I don't have any choice," Frannie grumbled. "People always said you were jealous of me. I should have believed them."

Miranda directed her laugh at the cute roll of fat above Frannie's jeans. "Why would *I* be jealous of *you*?"

"Because I have real friends now," Frannie said, "and you've got six more years of kissing Paisley's butt and hoping she doesn't ditch you the same way you ditched me."

"I didn't ditch you," Miranda muttered. "You said you never wanted to talk to me again. What was I supposed to say?"

"How about *I'm sorry, Frannie?*"

It was the perfect opportunity for Miranda to make things right.

Instead, she picked up the stapler.

Ca-chunk. Ca-chunk.

For the next three hours, that was the only sound in the theater. After a while it began to sound like the *click, clack, tick, tap* of texting in Whisper's story. What was the difference, really? The world was filled with monsters ready to get you. Some were mutant thumbs. Some were bloodthirsty killers. And some were former best friends.

CHAPTER 17

SOPHIE

Wednesday nights at the Wexler house meant it was Jade's turn to cook dinner. While she prepared in the kitchen, Mom and Dad lay on the couch giving each other foot rubs, and Sophie practiced piano.

"Is that *Danse Macabre?*" Mom asked.

"Mm-hmm," Sophie responded. Keeping it humble. For now.

"Doesn't sound like dance music to me," Dad joked.

"It does if you're a skeleton," Mom said. "*Danse Macabre* is about the figure of Death enticing skeletons to rise from their graves."

Graves. Death. The *thonk-thonk* that had Sophie and the girls running from the cemetery.

Sophie's right pinkie hit a sour note. Had that really been Silas Hoke? They'd been over it a dozen times at school that day and no one had a theory that made better sense.

"Five minutes until Mexican!" Jade shouted.

Mexican cuisine! Here was Sophie's chance to announce her latest triumph: a 115 percent score on today's Spanish test. Mom and Dad would be muy orgullosa. But no one was prouder than Sophie herself.

Yes, she had scored above perfect before. Billions of times. But this was different. She'd had to study all the way to Crimson Creek Cemetery. While terrified. It was beyond challenging. Even for her. And the worst part was that her parents would never know what she endured. Because what could Sophie possibly say? *Hey, Mom and Dad, last night I sat six feet above a dead guy who got squished to death by a roller coaster, then I was chased by the ghost of Silas Hoke. So, how was the Hoke Poke? Fun?*

Uh, no. No, she couldn't. Sophie would have to celebrate that victory alone.

"Four minutes!" Jade shouted.

Sophie tried to focus on the music, but Whisper's story clawed back into her mind. Suddenly she imagined each of her fingers detaching, hopping from key to key, finishing Camille Saint-Saëns's song much better than she could, while bright red blood splotched the white ivory.

"Three minutes!"

Thumbs.

An image of Guitar Guy picking and plucking his guitar strings popped into her mind. She couldn't imagine his black-polished thumbs separating from his hands. He was too confident, too commanding for that. He was a lot like Adrian in Whisper's story. Not because he didn't have a cell phone—he obviously did, or he wouldn't have been able to AirDrop his number—but because Adrian saved Agnes from herself, and Sophie had a feeling that Dane Jeremy might save her one day, too.

Dane Jeremy.

"Two minutes!"

Sophie had muttered the name to herself roughly *seventeen thousand* times. And on the seventeen-thousandth-and-*first* time, she'd realized that it sounded a lot like "Danger Me."

Was Dane Jeremy dangerous? Guys who stick gummy bears to windows were harmless, right? Sure, Ms. Drassel saw him as a threat, all right, but only to Sophie's playing. Not to her life.

"One minute!"

But Guitar Guy—Dane Jeremy—Danger Me—wasn't some mysterious rando. He and Sophie had been flirting through that studio window for months. Granted, they'd never spoken, but it was more than she'd ever communicated with the boys at school.

The final bar of *Danse Macabre* was clunky. Proof that Sophie's thumbs had other things on their squishy yellow minds. Things like texting Danger Me. She closed the piano. It echoed like the door of a tomb.

"¡La cena!" Jade said as the kitchen door flew open. The music of Diego El Cigala danced through the wireless speakers. Sophie's time in the spotlight was over. The Jade show was about to begin.

The kitchen table, Sophie had to admit, was beautifully set. A Mexican blanket served as a tablecloth, and each quesadilla had a tiny red-and-yellow flag stabbed into its center. A little much? Try a *lot* much. Yet Sophie found herself encouraged. When she broke the news of her 115 percent, everyone could wave their teeny flags in celebration.

Gracias, Jade, she thought.

They dug in. The food was, of course, A-plus.

"Smart choice swapping beef for shrimp." Mom was a dietary consultant; her praise carried weight. "And the caramelized vegetables offset the spiciness wonderfully— and without added fat."

Dad, an overworked financial advisor, didn't know a carb from a protein. "All I know is it's the best burrito I've ever had."

Mom and Jade laughed—it was a quesadilla! Sophie laughed, too. But only because she wanted everything to appear normal for when she reached into her back pocket and slapped her test on the table like a winning hand. Which she was just about to do.

"¿Sabes qué?" Jade asked.

Sophie's blood went gazpacho cold.

Anytime Jade started a conversation with *Guess what?*, she had big news. Asking in Spanish meant it would be even bigger.

Mom and Dad glanced at each other, smiling expectantly. Sophie left her quiz in her back pocket.

"Yo tengo buenas noticias," Jade said, her cheeks round with joy. "Señora Fritz, mi profesora de español, ¡me ofreció un trabajo de verano!"

Sophie's parents had picked up a little Spanish from their daughters, but not this much.

"Jade's Spanish teacher offered her a summer job," Sophie translated.

"No kidding," Dad said. "What kind?"

"¡Ayudándola a enseñar español!"

Mom and Dad turned to Sophie. Why did she have to be the bearer of Jade's good news?

"She's going to help teach Spanish immersion."

"¡En Sevilla!" Jade added.

"In Seville," Sophie muttered.

"¡España!" Jaded added.

"Spain," Sophie mumbled.

With an eek of delight, Mom leaped from her seat and pulled Jade up for a hug. Jade grinned with perfect teeth, so much so that her stylish glasses slid down her perfect nose. Dad went next, lifting Jade off her feet. Sophie watched joylessly. A flawless Spanish test versus *an actual job in Spain?* They'd never care. Still, she had to try.

"I got my Spanish test back today."

"Oh yeah?" Mom replied. "Maybe Señora Fritz will offer *you* a job one day, too."

"What kind of expenses are covered?" Dad asked Jade. "Not that it matters. We'll find a way to make it work."

Jade replied, but Sophie didn't hear it. Studying on the way to a graveyard. Acing the test. No, *beyond* acing the test. And a hypothetical job offer was all Sophie got? What did a straight A student have to do to get attention in this family? *Fail?*

Sophie giggled a little as she imagined failing just to get time in the spotlight. It was a ridiculous idea. A useless thought experiment. The most backward solution she could possibly find. And yet the thrill Sophie got from telling a bad story to the Grim Sleepers, from surprising them with her incompetence, could not be overlooked. Success had always come easy to her. Everyone expected it. But failing? That was hard. So why not challenge herself and get some much-needed attention from her parents while she was at it?

"I got an F," Sophie announced.

The conversation stopped.

"What do you mean, 'an F'?" Mom asked, genuinely perplexed.

"On my Spanish test," Sophie said.

"I don't understand," her father said.

"An F, Dad. It stands for *fail*."

Her parents traded confused looks.

"I don't understand," Dad said. "This was on a test?"

"Spanish."

"I can tutor her!" Jade announced. For once, everyone ignored her.

"Did you know about the test?" Mom asked.

"Yep."

"Did the teacher actually teach the material?"

"Yep."

"*Before* the test?"

"Yep."

Mom placed her palm on Sophie's forehead. "You're a little warm. Are you feeling okay?"

"Never better."

"Were you distracted?" Mom asked. "Was someone bothering you?"

"Nope," Sophie said. "I just got an F."

For the rest of dinner, the conversation was shifted off Jade's summer in Seville and onto Sophie's unprecedented failure. Why she thought it happened. What she could do differently. If she'd had any big fights with her friends. If stealing attention from a sister were a school subject, Sophie would be on her way to Seville with a lesson plan right now.

Her failure was a total success. She'd jumped from the plane and allowed herself to fall. Only, she hadn't crashed. She'd soared. For her next jump, maybe she'd text Danger Me. What's the worst that could happen? Her parents would find out she was texting a mysterious boy? Then what? They'd get mad at her? Punish her? Yell?

Perfect.

CHAPTER 18

ZUZU

Zuzu slithered through the stream of middle schoolers and tucked herself into the water fountain nook. It was Thursday. Fourth period. Paisley and Miranda were at the other end of the hall—the farthest they'd been from Zuzu all day. She could finally deliver her urgent message without being spotted. Once her place in the Grim Sleepers was more secure, she'd work to change Gemma's no-texting-about-Grim-Sleepers rule. *What is this, a 1980s horror flick?* Cell phones existed for a reason.

The bathroom door shut behind Gemma and Whisper. Zuzu slipped a red marker and her (not-leather!) journal from her bag and wrote:

OUT OF ORDER

She ripped out the page, then grabbed the wad of cinnamon gum she'd been chewing and smooshed it to the back of the paper. When no one was looking, she stuck it to the door and slipped inside.

After dragging the trash can in front of the door and checking her outfit in the mirror—denim jumpsuit, white platform high-tops, refreshed purple streak (perfection!)—Zuzu peeked under the stalls. Targets confirmed: Gemma's clogs and Whisper's (probably vegan) running shoes. Ideally, Sophie and Frannie would have been there, too, but Zuzu didn't have time for ideal. If Paisley and Miranda knew she was sneaking off to collude with their archenemies, they'd put a text hex on her.

"Did Tina freak when she saw your hair?" Gemma asked Whisper.

She was referring to the new strands of pink hair poking from beneath Whisper's beanie. Did Whisper credit Zuzu for the inspiration? Of course not. No one ever did. According to Zuzu's mother, *A good influencer plants a seed of inspiration, then flits away. The client must believe they fashioned the idea by themselves.* The job was thankless but gratifying. A blessing and a curse. More time spent in the shadows.

"*Freak* is an understatement," Whisper replied. "She told me it better be gone before my dad gets back from his business trip or else."

"Or else *what?*"

"Exactly." Whisper flushed the toilet. "What's she going to do? Tell my mom?"

Zuzu grinned. She had a soft spot for dark humor.

"She did say I have to do all of Paisley's chores until I wash it out."

Gemma flushed. "That's hella Cinderella."

"Yeah. Me scrubbing floors while Paisley gets her claws manicured—"

"Sorry to interrupt," Zuzu interrupted, "but we have to go back!"

The stall doors opened.

"Zuzu!" Gemma cried. "Will you please stop creeping up on us?"

"Go back *where?*" Whisper asked.

"The pink elevates your vibe, by the way," Zuzu said. "Totally worth a few extra chores if you ask me." Which, of course, no one had.

Whisper smiled at her own reflection. "Right?"

"Right," Zuzu said. "I'm also right about going back. To Crimson Creek Cemetery."

Gemma added, as she pumped soap, "I'm literally washing my hands of that place."

"What if that *thonk-thonk* we heard was Hoke?" Zuzu pressed. "The *real* Hoke?"

"Exactly," Whisper said. "What if it was? Do we really want to go back—"

Thud. The trash can. Someone was at the bathroom door.

"Read the sign!" Zuzu shouted.

"Z?" Paisley called. "Is that you?"

Desperate, Zuzu turned to the sinks, wrenched the handles so the faucets were pouring water at full blast, and, in her deepest voice, said, "Out of order, kid." Then, to Gemma: "Bring your G-Tone! I mean, charge it first, and actually read the manual, but come on! Tomorrow *is* the one hundredth anniversary of Hoke's electrocution. Now's our chance!"

"To what?" Whisper asked. "Lose a leg? *Die?*"

"Sorry, Zuzu. But we have plans tomorrow night," Gemma said.

Whisper turned off the faucets. "We do?"

"We're going to Ashgate Prison."

"We *are?*"

"Why would you do that?" Zuzu asked. "The whole town will be there for the parade."

"Outside the prison, maybe." Gemma hit the hand dryer. "But we're going *inside*. When Silas's ghost starts moaning about being electrocuted, we'll be there with my G-Tone. And yes, it's charged."

"We *will*?" Whisper asked.

Zuzu stood beside Gemma's dryer, her purple hair flying all over. "You don't think you'll get a better recording at the cemetery? Where Hoke is actually buried?"

"No one's asking me," Whisper said, "but I think we'll get *killed* at the cemetery."

Knuckles rapped on the door. Paisley's voice: "Let us in!"

Zuzu brought a silencing finger to her lips. Whisper and Gemma nodded. As the knocking persisted, Zuzu found herself gazing into the mirror. She was struck by how different they each looked. How unique. Gemma with those big blue eyes, bell-bottom jeans, and a scarf tied around her head. Whisper with her white beanie, glasses, an oversize sweatshirt, and tattered sneakers. And Zuzu, a glossy page from Jōhin's fall catalogue. They were like a band of superheroes—each with her own costume and powers. Each forced to conceal a true identity from the unsuspecting masses. If only they could reach beyond their comfort zones and overcome their fears. The Grim Sleepers could be horror heroes!

The knocking continued.

Zuzu had to make her final pitch, fast.

"If you want to level up your club, you're going to have to do next-level things."

Gemma scowled. "Our club *is* next-level."

Zuzu held up her journal. "I have ideas. Tons of them!"

"We already have *ideas*."

The fifth-period bell rang. It was now or never.

"I think you're afraid to go back to the cemetery," Zuzu dared.

Gemma crossed her arms. "And I think you're afraid to be seen with us in public."

Ouch. Zuzu wanted to push back, but what could she say? The trash can against the door said it all.

Without another word, Whisper and Gemma slid the trash can aside and left, leaving Zuzu alone, a horror superhero without a single sidekick.

As she hurried to catch up with Paisley and Miranda, Zuzu couldn't help wondering if Gemma was right. Maybe she wasn't as brave as she thought.

CHAPTER 19

SILAS HOKE

This town does a lot of stupid things to try to scare me off.

Monday's Hoke Stoke. I took care of that with a thunderstorm.

Tuesday's Hoke Poke. Let those idiots stab themselves with needles all they want.

Wednesday's Hoke Soak. Moronic. I wasn't afraid of water. I was afraid of amputation.

But tonight's Hoke Smoke barbecue?

I like this one.

There are carnival games. Even a few rickety rides. (Sorry, Obert. Too soon?)

The girls I've been watching are here.

Look at them.

Whisper and Frannie riding the Tilt-A-Whirl.

Sophie and Gemma throwing darts at balloons.

They're having fun.

Did I ever have fun? Even once?

Yes. Once. Ginny Baker.

The games and the rides are not what I like about the Thursday-night Hoke Smoke, anyway.

I like the barbecue.

The sweet smell of cooked flesh permeates the fairgrounds.

It makes me think of my own flesh, zapped to perfection by Old Sparky.

I wonder if these girls will eat barbecue and make this comparison, too.

Well, not the vegetarian.

Look, there's Paisley and Miranda.

Dang it. They see me. They're motioning me over.

I guess I need to switch back into Zuzu mode for a while.

Don't worry, Silas Hoke.

We'll be together again tomorrow night.

On the anniversary of your burial.

At the graveyard.

CHAPTER 20

FRANNIE

Frannie yawned.

The only thing worse than being seated between Paisley and Miranda was being seated between Paisley and Miranda in Mr. Melton's science class during last period on a Friday. The upside was that Frannie didn't dare look left (Miranda) or right (Paisley). This offered her no option other than to focus on Mr. Melton and give him the impression that she was a budding biologist hanging on his every word.

Which wasn't easy. Everyone called him Mr. Melatonin because he put his students to sleep. Even his clothes were boring. Beige on beige with a splash of beige. The best Frannie could do was focus on his hair, which sprouted from every bit of exposed skin except the top of his head.

It was kind of like he ate a gorilla that was now escaping through any opening it could find.

"Cells are the building blocks of all living things," he blathered. "The human body is composed of trillions of them. They provide structure for the body, convert nutrients into energy, and a zillion other of the dullest things you've ever heard in your life."

Okay, Frannie made up that last part. It did get her thinking, though. What happened to the cells inside Silas Hoke's body when Old Sparky finally electrocuted him?

She imagined them glowing red hot and exploding like fireworks. Then darkness. At least, she *hoped* it had ended in darkness. Because at midnight tonight, she and the girls were going to Ashgate Prison to record his ghostly groans on Gemma's G-Tone, and Frannie wasn't sure if she wanted to hear him or not.

As she weighed the likelihood of hearing something, a crumpled piece of paper landed beside her zebra-striped sneakers.

"Psst."

Miranda's *psst*. Frannie knew it well. She thought of the notes they used to pass in Ms. Boylan's class. The memory hurt. But it didn't have to. Frannie could use this as an opportunity to *fuse*. Not for Miranda's sake. Not even for her own.

For the play.

Frannie reached into her jeans pocket and, for courage, rubbed one of the silky Jōhin handkerchiefs Zuzu had given her. It was as if the handkerchiefs had been infused with everything that made Zuzu so confident. Maybe those qualities could rub off on Frannie.

"Psst." Miranda tried again. Her yellow-tinted computer glasses were fixed on Frannie. She jutted her chin at the crumpled-up paper and mouthed *Paisley.*

Frannie leaned down, plucked up the crumpled ball, and held it out to Paisley.

"Is that a *note*, Ms. Vargas-Stein?"

Frannie froze.

"Now *this* is exciting!" Mr. Melatonin said, his dull eyes uncharacteristically bright. "A good old-fashioned paper note! Pay heed, class. This is how we used to do it before texting took the excitement out of secret messages." He opened his hairy hand and walked toward her, shoes squeaking. "May I see it?"

Frannie's face started to burn. "Uh, no, that's okay."

"Oh, you simply must," he said. "The passed notes of my youth were such fun! *Will you go to the homecoming dance with me? Jenny likes your older brother. I'm going to beat you up after school.*" He sighed wistfully and wiggled his hairy fingers at the note.

Miranda coughed, *"Swallow it!"*

Frannie considered it, but her mouth was too dry, her throat too thick with fear.

"Now, Ms. Vargas-Stein."

There was no way out of this. She handed over the note.

As Mr. Melatonin uncrumpled it, Frannie's heart throbbed so furiously that she could feel it in her scalp.

"How does Mr. Melatonin breathe with all that nose hair?" he read.

The whole class laughed—minus Frannie, Miranda, and Paisley.

Mr. Melatonin's delighted smile began to harden. Then crack. The teacher no longer looked boring. He looked evil. If only Zuzu were there. She'd know exactly what horror movie to compare him to.

"Well." Mr. Melatonin exhaled through his nose like a dragon. "This note isn't fun at *all.* Did you write this?"

Frannie just sat there, her burning flesh puddling into goo. Now what? She could tell the truth and destroy any potential theater bond she might create with Miranda. Or she could lie, shoulder the blame, and *fuse.*

"I wrote it," Frannie said. "I'm sorry."

Mr. Melatonin shook his head in grave disappointment. "Betrayed by my star pupil!"

Frannie's heart sank into her zebra-striped sneakers.

"Since you're so curious about how I get my oxygen, Ms. Vargas-Stein," he said, "I'd like you here Monday morning, seven o'clock sharp, to help me prep frogs for dissection. I'll be breathing the whole time. You'll be fascinated."

Frannie thought of Whisper's story, how Agnes's thumbs had revolted while cutting open a frog. The whole class had laughed at her, just as they were laughing at Frannie now. Just like they'd laughed when Frannie peed her jeans. She might keep her thumbs, but not her dignity.

By the end of fifth period, Frannie's belly felt full of humiliation bricks. Or maybe they were anger bricks, or regret bricks, or I-loathe-Miranda bricks. Whatever they were, they weighed neither Miranda nor Paisley down one bit. When the bell rang, they sprang from their seats and bolted for the exit faster than one could say *pure evil.*

"You're welcome, by the way," Frannie snapped when she spotted Miranda in the pickup line after school. Despite the autumn chill, Frannie was still boiling hot.

"For what?" Miranda said, violet-blue eyes wide with innocence.

"Um, for taking the blame for you? For letting Mr. Melatonin hate me instead of you? For getting a *detention*?"

Miranda scoffed. "Yeah, that was dumb. Why'd you do that?"

"For you!" Frannie exploded. "For us! For the play!"

Miranda scowled. "Stop trying to fix things, Frannie. I'm never going to forgive you."

"Forgive *me*? Why would *you* have to forgive *me*?"

Miranda crossed her arms. "Two words for you. *Theater. Group.*"

"I only auditioned because you asked me to! It was your idea."

"Because I was there all the time!" Miranda exploded. "I thought if we were in the same company, we could hang out more! I didn't think you'd take over!"

"I didn't take over. When I was offered the lead in *Hairspray*, I asked if you cared. You said no. You told me to take it! You said you weren't mad!"

"What else was I supposed to say?"

"How about the truth?"

"What truth? That you were chubby and that's the only reason they thought you'd make a good Tracy Turnblad?"

Oof. Frannie felt that one right in the heart. Not because it was true but because Miranda was *that* cruel.

"And you think I got Audrey only because DayNa likes me, right?"

"Right."

"Wrong," Frannie snipped. "I get these roles because I'm a better actress, singer, and dancer than you. End. Scene."

Was it an obnoxious thing to say? Yes. Was Frannie a bragger? Never. But Miranda had thrown the first punch—actually, the first ten rounds of punches—and Frannie was tired of standing there, allowing herself to get hit.

"No wonder Paisley is your only friend," she added, hoping for a knockout.

"Um, Paisley is *not* my only friend. I have Zuzu and—"

"Zuzu?" Frannie laughed. "If she likes you so much, why is she sneaking off and hanging out with me?"

The car pickup line was not a quiet place. Car horns honked, kids shouted, music blared. Yet everything suddenly felt suffocatingly quiet.

Had Frannie just betrayed Zuzu's secret? Yes. Yes, she had. But in that moment, the pained confusion on Miranda's face made it all feel worth it.

"You *wish* Zuzu was hanging out with you," Miranda fired back weakly.

Frannie wanted to end it there. Needed to end it there. She'd already said too much. But she'd been victimized for too long. Now that she'd started punching, she couldn't stop.

"I don't have to *wish*, Miranda. Zuzu and I were together Tuesday night, and we'll probably hang out this weekend." Frannie shrugged. "I guess you're not as close as you thought you were."

Knockout!

Miranda's mother pulled up to the curb.

"I don't believe you," Miranda said as she reached for the car door.

"Enjoy your one friend," Frannie called as she walked to the bike racks, the clear winner.

Or was she? Winning usually made Frannie feel buoyant and light. Not weak-kneed and overcome with flu-like symptoms. Not *mean*.

Was this how Miranda felt all the time?

Worse than hurting Miranda was that Frannie had betrayed Zuzu. She shuddered at what those girls would do to Zuzu once they confirmed she was sneaking around behind their backs. And she double-shuddered to think what Zuzu would do to Frannie for exposing her secret.

Overcome with panic, Frannie paused by her bike and reached into her pocket to touch the Jōhin silk. She needed comfort, reassurance, a soft place to land.

But it was gone.

CHAPTER 21

SOPHIE

Sophie had been going to the Hoke Folk with her family since she was in her mother's belly, and she wasn't allowed to stop now. The Wexlers listened to the mayor's address together. They admired the floats together. They marched to the prison together. They went home and drank hot chocolate together. But tonight, the Grim Sleepers had a plan that would require Sophie to separate from her family, just for a little while. If she didn't get caught—or killed—everything would be fine.

With the entire town and almost twice its population in tourists waiting breathlessly behind him, Mayor Chakrabarti stood on the top stair of the town square pavilion, watching the sun shave down to a single razor of light over the horizon. The second it dipped under—the instant it was officially dusk—he turned to the restless crowd.

"For one hundred years it has been a local tradition to parade to Ashgate Prison at dusk on the anniversary of Silas Hoke's death. And why do we do this?"

"Unity," Jade called as if being tested.

Dad pulled her closer, never tiring of her perfection.

"That's right!" the mayor called, his voice magnifying across the square. "It's a show of unity. It's also proof that the people of Misery Falls band together to . . ."

"Defeat evil!" everyone shouted.

"Yes! And who is evil?"

"Silas Hoke!" Sophie shouted along with the crowd.

"Now, who's ready to go to Ashgate Prison and show Silas Hoke what the good people of Misery Falls are all about?"

A cacophony of whooping swelled across the town square as the crowd took to the streets behind their strutting grand marshal.

Flanked by her parents and cushioned by the masses, Sophie danced her way down the block, propelled by the up-tempo trumpeting of the Misery Falls High School marching band.

Ahhhh, the power of music.

Ahhhh, instruments.

Ahhhh, Danger Me!

It didn't matter what Sophie was doing or who she was doing it with. All week, all thoughts had led to Dane Jeremy. Disruptor of piano lessons! God of the gummies! Haver of adorable hair!

What if his name sounded like Danger Me on purpose? What if he was a Hoke henchman, there to lure her into a trap? Or a grisly old plastic surgeon who swapped his face with that of a cute teen boy so he could distract Sophie from her piano lessons and free Ms. Drassel up to teach someone more punctual?

But what if Danger Me saw something different in Sophie that no one else did?

A spark. A crackle. A glint. A Danger Sophie—a Danger *Phie*. If only there were a textbook she could read or a teacher she could ask.

While dancing their way to the prison, it was impossible for Sophie to ignore the guys stealing glances at Jade. She was pretty in an unfair sort of way. A fetching mess of soft curls framed her face like it was a work of art. When teeth don't need braces, lashes don't need mascara, and skin doesn't need zit cream, Mother Nature goes the extra mile to protect it. Yes, Jade had glasses, but they were thick black ones. The kind that girls who

don't need glasses wear anyway. The kind that boys at parades find attractive.

Was Jade aware of her magnetism? It was hard to say. Years of popularity had trained her to act humble. Surely, though, all that attention had taught her a thing or two about playing the game. What if Jade could help?

"Can I ask you a question?" Sophie shouted above the elephantine horns.

"You want to go to Spain with me, don't you?"

"Uh, no."

"It's okay, Soph. I know it's going to be weird when I'm gone, but—"

"Has a random boy ever given you his number before?"

"Oh." Jade paused as silver confetti rained down on them. She gave Sophie an expertly honed *look at my face, of course they have* expression. "Why?"

Sophie shrugged. "Did you text him?"

"You mean *them*." Jade pulled a silver fleck from her eyelashes and released it into the crowd. "Ew! No. I would never."

"Why not?"

"I'm too young to die."

An oversize black balloon sailed toward Sophie. She gave it a backhanded whack. "Why does everyone

assume strangers are dangerous? Most violent crimes are committed by someone close to the victim."

"Exactly," Jade said. "So why let anyone get close?"

Dang it. She was good. Sophie tried again.

"Technically everyone's a stranger until you get to know them."

Jade cocked her head. "I suppose. But if a guy wants to hang and doesn't even know me, then he's only interested in my looks. And I'm more than that." Jade gave Sophie a glance. "We both are."

Jade meant well. But someone who didn't know Sophie Wexler was exactly what Sophie Wexler needed!

Danger Me wasn't impressed by her perfect grades. Her extracurriculars. Her bid for student council president. All he knew was that Sophie had big curls, warm brown eyes, and a dimple that showed up on the left side of her chin when she smiled. He knew she played piano but had no idea she played well. So yeah. Right now, Danger Me probably *did* like Sophie only for her face. Why was that such a bad thing? Maybe Jade was bored by this sort of attention. But it was new to Sophie. She didn't have to succeed to get it. She didn't even have to fail to get it. She didn't have to do a single thing!

"What if you *kind* of knew him? Would you text him? And if so, what would you say?"

"Talk to me," Jade demanded. "Who is he?"

Sophie flashed a coy smile. The same kind she used when she didn't want her friends to guess what she'd bought for their birthday . . . but also kind of did.

"Spill it!" Jade cried.

"Spill what?" Mom shouted above the music.

"Nothing," Sophie said as she danced a little to the left, putting some distance between them and their parents. Softer, to Jade, she said, "I met him at JAM, okay?"

"Well, unmeet him," Jade said, cutting a look at their mom—a silent promise to snitch if Sophie didn't comply. "JAM takes students from all over, not just Misery Falls. He could be from anywhere." The black balloon pitched toward her. She punched it back into the crowd. "What's going on with you? First you get an F in Spanish. Now this? It's like you're *trying* to get into trouble."

"Why would I want to do that?" Sophie asked innocently.

"Same reason you'd text a stranger. You're crying out for help."

"No, Jade, I'm crying out for *fun!*"

The music stopped, the dancing slowed, and the balloons settled as everyone gathered around the locked gates of Ashgate Prison. Over the years there had been talk of converting the dilapidated brick prison into a movie theater or apartments, but no one wanted to develop a

haunted property. It just sat there, abandoned and alone, waiting for approval that never came.

Sophie knew the feeling.

Mayor Chakrabarti stepped onto a riser and waited for silence.

"Ladies and gentlemen," he began, "please join me in our traditional chant to keep evil spirits away from Misery Falls for one more year!"

That was Sophie's cue.

"I have to go to the bathroom," she announced. Faster than her mother could say *hold it*, Sophie called, "Be back soon!"

As she worked her way through the crowd, the mayor began the chant.

"Unclean spirits, depart our lovely town!"

"Unclean spirits, depart our lovely town!" everyone echoed.

"Ghosts risen up, go back down!"

"Ghosts risen up, go back down!"

"In your powers we respectfully believe!"

"In your powers we respectfully believe!"

"But we, the Hoke folk, command you to leave!"

"But we, the Hoke folk, command you to leave!"

Sophie snuck around the back of the prison to the sounds of hundreds of people cheering as the band struck up a victory song.

Without all the people, without the protection of parents, the building seemed to transform into a haunted house. The sagging roof gave the structure Dracula's hunched shoulders. Shards of glass in broken windows glowed in the moonlight, white as fangs. Weeds and vines strangled the building like they were trying to drag it into the abyss.

Sophie's throat turned to sandpaper.

Were they really going inside?

Needing a distraction, Sophie took out her phone. If she was going to text Danger Me, the time was now, because nothing could be more dangerous than what she was about to do.

Sophie scrolled to the contact she'd labeled DANGER ME and texted:

Hi.

The moment she hit Send, her adrenaline surged, and she began to pace. "Ohmigod, ohmigod, ohmigod!" *Did I just do that?*

Hands shaking, she waited for the three glorious dots to appear.

Nothing.

Maybe he didn't see it. She tried again.

> **What R U doing?**

Still nothing. Oh wait—He didn't have her number. He probably had no idea who was texting.

One more time.

> **It's me Sophie. From JAM. I play piano.**

No response.

No surprise.

What made Sophie believe a guitar guy with black nail polish, a blond hair streak, and vintage concert T-shirts would have a crush on her? She was Sophie, not Jade.

Gemma materialized from the darkness with a bag slung over her shoulder and holding her G-Tone like an Uzi. Sophie stuffed her phone in her pocket. Yep, they were really doing this.

When Whisper and Frannie arrived, they texted their parents as planned. Sophie's text read:

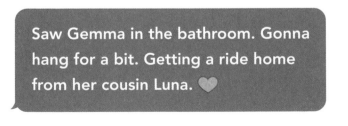

> **Saw Gemma in the bathroom. Gonna hang for a bit. Getting a ride home from her cousin Luna.** 💜

Ready? Gemma mouthed as she powered on the G-Tone. Sophie, Whisper, and Frannie nodded, too afraid to speak.

Sophie wanted to tell them she'd texted Danger Me and he'd ghosted her. If only so they could lift her spirits with one of their patented Relax Attacks. But she was embarrassed, ashamed, confused. It was the first time Sophie had tried for something and failed. Like, *really* tried and *really* failed. This time, the F was real.

The good news? If Sophie didn't make it out of this prison alive, she wouldn't have to face Danger Me on Tuesday.

So it wasn't all bad.

CHAPTER 22

GEMMA

The night Whisper told her story at Crimson Creek Cemetery, nature had set the spooky scene: cloudy, foggy, with storm clouds rolling in. Tonight, though, none of the clichés had assembled to heighten the tension. There was a bright crescent moon. Starry skies. Clear visibility. Nowhere to hide.

All the better to hear you with, my dear, Gemma thought as she checked the charge light on her G-Tone. For the hundredth time. Still green.

She looked up to see Sophie peeking at her phone. "I *said*, no devices. I don't want your cellular frequency messing with the G-Tone's audio receptors."

Was that even a thing? Gemma had no idea. But it sounded legit, and she was tired of reminding Sophie that Grim Sleepers gatherings were device free.

"Who are you texting, anyway?" Frannie asked. "We're all here."

"I'm using it as a flashlight," Sophie lied. Or so Gemma suspected. Sophie's eyes were wide, and the corners of her mouth got stiff as a ventriloquist's dummy when she lied. She'd make a terrible spy.

"We don't need flashlights." Gemma patted her duffel bag. "I brought our candles."

Whisper began a protest. "Candles are fun when we're telling stories, but in the prison, maybe a flashlight—"

BLEE-OOP! BLEE-OOP!

Gemma gasped. "I've got something!"

"You sure that's not the charge alarm?" Frannie asked.

"That was a *SKRONG!*" Gemma cried. "This is a *BLEE-OOP!*"

The girls gaped at one another, then up at the brick building.

Gemma stepped closer and glanced back at the girls. "Come on."

Was she terrified? Beyond. But Gemma was the bravery glue holding this club together. Without her, they'd fall apart. And this club could not fall apart. The Grim Sleepers respected Gemma. She was their leader. They looked up to her, not down. Unlike her family.

Ugh, family.

Gemma had no choice but to get inside the prison. One recording of Silas Hoke and her family would forget all about that gigantic crate in the alley behind the store. Maybe they'd even buy a new cash register. Was it worth facing whatever was waiting for her inside this prison? She seriously hoped so.

The crowd sounds on the other side of the building were dissipating as everyone headed home. Fewer chances of getting caught; fewer chances of being saved. The closer Gemma edged toward the prison, the faster the lights strobed. *Something is in there. Stay close and follow me,* she wanted to say. All she could manage was "Follow."

The foursome clustered together like a giant spider, their eight legs creeping toward the boarded-up back door.

"It doesn't look like we can get inside," Whisper said.

"Yeah, if we disturb the police tape, someone might notice," Frannie said.

"That's okay. We're not going through the door," Gemma said. She had walked the perimeter before the sun went down. "Follow me."

Between rusted fence rails, through gnarled weeds, and on to the crumbled back entrance they went.

"That window." Gemma pointed. "There's a loose board. Whisper, you're up."

"Me?" she screeched. "Why me?"

"You're the smallest."

"I'm not small," Whisper protested. "I'm *muscular*."

"All the more reason."

"Zuzu is smaller than me."

"Yeah, well, she's not here, is she?" Gemma asked, aware of the bitterness in her voice. But come on. Zuzu had crashed one gathering. One! And then she thought she could swoop into the girls' bathroom and tell Gemma how and where the Grim Sleepers should be Hoke hunting? Yeah, no.

"Maybe we'd better do this when she's available," Whisper said.

"Nice try," Gemma said.

"She's probably mad at us," Frannie said.

"Why would she be mad at us?" Gemma replied. "She's the one who tried to take over."

"I dunno," Frannie said. "Maybe Miranda found out Zuzu was hanging with us. And maybe Zuzu thinks one of us told her. Not that I did. Not that any of us did."

"Dramatic much?" Sophie asked.

"Dramatic *always*," she fired back.

"None of us told Miranda anything," Gemma snapped. "Zuzu isn't here because she wanted to go to the cemetery tonight and hang out with her *real* friends." Gemma didn't say what she was really thinking: *I knew she wouldn't stick around. Cool girls like that never do.* "Now, Whisper, are you going to squeeze your muscular body through that window or not?"

"Not if you keep size-shaming me."

"How about if I coward-shame you instead?"

Whisper had been carrying herself a little more proudly since her superstar turn telling the thumb story. If Gemma was right, she knew Whisper wouldn't risk ruining that credibility. Even if it meant being torn to ribbons by broken glass, gnawed to gristle by rats, and dismembered by a one-legged ghost.

Gemma was right. Without another word, Whisper hoisted herself onto the rotten windowsill, wiggled her way under a loose board, and landed with a dense *thud.*

"Are you in?"

"Unfortunately," Whisper called. Her voice was distant and small. "It smells like dust and burnt hair. I can't see anything. Can I please turn on my—"

"No! Someone might see!" Gemma warned. "Pull off the board and we'll come in. I have candles."

Seconds later: *Thack!* The board shot through the window and landed on a patch of dead grass.

Nice kick! Gemma wanted to say. But talking while terrified was a skill she had yet to master. Instead she

tumbled silently through the window with Frannie and Sophie following.

Inside, darkness swallowed them whole. Gemma felt for her duffel and unzipped it with a slithering sound. Candles clunked like rolling bones. Her fingers found the matches and scratched one to life. Gradually, a flickering orange view of her own hands emerged as she lit and handed out four candles.

Cobwebs stretched against them like skin before ripping away like, well, severed legs. The taste of pennies flooded Gemma's mouth. She was going to puke, or pass out, or both. She tried to focus on her candle's flame. The flickering was hypnotic. It brought warmth to the frigid and forgotten hallway and cast shadows across the—

Whisper gasped.

Then Frannie.

Then Sophie.

The flames illuminated two words written on ash-gray cinderblocks.

HOKE LIVES

Whisper began to whimper. "Nail polish!" she stammered. "Just like—in my story—"

"Why would prisoners have nail polish?!" Sophie cried.

"It's not nail polish," Frannie quaked. "It's blood."

They screamed again.

"Stop!" Gemma demanded. "If someone hears, we could get arrested! It's probably just paint." *Please, my angels and guardians, let it be paint.*

The G-Tone began to flash red. Gemma's breath hitched. "This thing's going crazy."

She waved the device though the air. When she directed it toward the deeper dark of the prison, the lights blinked faster. "It's picking up audio. Sounds we can't hear."

Frannie grabbed Gemma's arm. "What's it saying?"

"I dunno. I have to upload the recording to the Borderlyne app."

"Hold on," Sophie said. "We have no way of knowing what it's picking up? How is that helpful?"

"That's not good!" Whisper was squirming like someone barely holding in a pee. "It could be saying, *Leave now or I'm going to make stilts out of all your legs.*"

"We don't leave until it stops communicating," Gemma insisted. "This recording could change our lives."

"Or end them," Frannie said.

"Stop panicking," Gemma urged. Their panicking was making her panic. "We're protected by angels and guardians. I promise."

But were they really? Suddenly the ghost of Silas Hoke felt a lot more real than any of the other mystical beings Gemma believed in.

Chunks of collapsed ceiling crunched like teeth beneath their shoes as the girls entered the prison block. Wide and open, the two-story area gave way to dozens of empty graffiti-scrawled cells. At least, Gemma *hoped* they were empty.

The G-Tone's pulsating lights led the way through the cellblock and down a dark narrow hall.

Death row.

With the help of the flickering candles, the girls came upon a closed door and more red graffiti. Or nail polish. Or blood.

OLD SPARKY

The girls gasped, flapped their hands, ran in tight circles. This was it! The room with the electric chair. The room where Hoke died exactly one hundred years ago. The room where he swore he'd be back.

Gemma's muscles tightened. "We should probably go in, right?" *Wrong! Wrong! Wrong!* Still she crept toward the door, breathing in short bursts as the girls huddled behind her. On the count of three, she yanked the knob.

The hinges gave the guttural moan of a beast rising from the ocean depths.

There, barely visible in the candlelight, waited Old Sparky.

It was constructed of old brown wood. Nearly black— most likely from burning flesh. Leather straps, limp and exhausted, dangled down the sides. A metal cap hung over the top, suspended by a coiled electric cable that fed into the ceiling.

"I can't believe it's still here," Sophie whispered, awestruck.

The lights on the G-Tone had gone solid red. Not that Gemma needed a gadget to tell her they weren't alone. She felt the weight of another being all over her body like frost on her bones. Was it Silas Hoke or the collective energy of every criminal who'd been electrocuted in this chair?

Then a sound like a fuse being blown.

Pop!

Gemma's stomach lurched.

"He's here!" Frannie peeped.

Pop!

"We're leaving," Whisper trembled. "For real this time!"

"Agreed!" Sophie cried.

Ignoring them, Gemma moved closer to Old Sparky. She was dragging Frannie with her. "This is our chance!"

"Stop," Frannie begged. "This is getting—"

Pop!

"Gemma!" Whisper shouted. "Let's go!"

"Not yet! We need a clean recording! I have a crate of G-Tones to sell!"

Then the door slammed shut and a dark figure emerged.

CHAPTER 23

WHISPER

Pop!

"Zuzu? Seriously?" Whisper said. "Again?"

"What?" Zuzu asked, feigning innocence. Though her outfit—black denim cutoffs over ripped black tights, combat boots, and a Freddy Krueger T-shirt concealed by a leather moto jacket—was anything but.

"I hope that's fake leather," Whisper said as her raging heartbeat began to slow.

"I already posted it on eBay," Zuzu said. "This is our last hurrah."

Satisfied, Whisper smiled. Never did she imagine telling Zuzu Otsuka what to do with her leather. Never *ever* did she think Zuzu Otsuka would actually do it.

"What do you mean, 'what'?" Gemma said, getting back to business. "Enough with the jump scares, Zuzu. That's not what we're about."

"I wasn't trying to scare you this time," she insisted. "I was just following you."

"Well, you didn't have to. We *invited* you to come."

Zuzu peered down at her midnight-blue fingernail polish. "I'm used to hiding in the shadows, I guess."

"Said the girl with, like, a billion followers," Frannie snipped, sounding the tiniest bit jealous.

"That's different," Zuzu said. Then, to Gemma: "You were right. This is where we should be on the anniversary of Silas Hoke's death. The cemetery is better for *tomorrow* night, the anniversary of his *burial*."

Gemma's clenched jaw softened.

Whisper's hardened. Did they really have to go back there?

"Well." Sophie exhaled. "At least we know the blood on the walls isn't real."

Zuzu drew back her head, more disappointed than surprised. "What do you mean it's not real?"

"Didn't you do that? To scare us?"

"No." Zuzu raised her right hand. "I swear." She blew a bubble with her signature cinnamon gum.

Pop!

The G-Tone lit up.

"Noooo." Gemma slumped against a wall. "What if the G-Tone was just picking up your gum this whole time?"

Whisper welcomed that theory, sort of. Believing they were surrounded by talking spirits was horrifying. It was also promising. If the G-Tone could record the voices of executed inmates, maybe it could deliver a message from other dead people, too.

Like her mom.

Tzzzz!

The dusty old light bulb above Old Sparky stuttered on with a *snick* of electricity.

Then off.

"Uh . . . you guys . . ."

The light bulb flickered on again.

The girls reached for one another.

"Zuzu," Whisper said, eyes fixed on that bulb. "Are you sure—"

"Yes, I'm sure. I'm an influencer, not an electrician."

"What if Hoke *became* electricity?" Frannie asked nervously.

"Electronic devices *do* talk to each other," Gemma breathed.

"Really?" Sophie took out her phone. "Let me check."

"Don't you dare!"

Whisper thought of her story: the severed thumbs using phones to communicate.

Was it possible?

Another flash. The bulb's insectile snicking seemed to be mocking them now.

"Shhhh." Gemma held the G-Tone up to the bulb. "I'm gonna try and get a clean—"

Boom! The bulb exploded.

There was probably screaming. There had to be. All Whisper knew for sure was that she was running—everyone was. How else would their candles have burned out? Running from death row, across the echoey cellblock, through another dark hallway, their speed causing the candles to blow out one by one.

There was stumbling behind her. Collisions. Slapping sneakers. Crumbling concrete. Maybe even the *thonk-thonk-thonk-thonk-thonk-thonk* of Hoke's leg.

Whisper was first through the window. Police tape stretched against her forehead. She fell, rolled across broken concrete. Her cheek scraped against brittle brown grass. She heard the others' frenzied footsteps. They were okay.

She leaped up, trampled through the weeds, slipped between the rusty fence rails, and bolted across the empty street. The town square was a blur of panic and tears.

But Whisper's track training kicked in, powered by pure muscle memory. She kept running, running, closer and closer to home.

Home. The thought of it heavied her heart. She never should have left. Correction: she never should have been *able* to leave. She was grounded! Tina should have been guarding her prisoner, yet she didn't even care enough to enforce Whisper's punishment.

Staggering from a stitch in her side, Whisper slowed to a jog on Hemlock Lane.

Bright light instantly blasted her—Old Sparky's bulbs, floating like ghosts and gaining strength, just like all those severed thumbs. Whisper pulled her beanie low.

"Don't hurt me! I'm sorry!"

The lights continued to blaze, but that was it. Her legs were still intact. She slowly rolled back the beanie to find headlights from an idling car. A Prius with the license plate 123RISE.

It was the name of her mother's bakery. It was her mother's car.

Mom?

Had the G-Tone somehow summoned her?

The driver opened the door and stepped onto Hemlock Lane.

It was not Jenny Martin.

It was Tina Pollard.

"Whisper!" Tina hurried toward her. "Where were you? Why are you running? Are you okay?"

Breathless, Whisper's chest heaved. She snuck out of the house. Broke her punishment. Trespassed in a broken-down prison. Was chased out by an electric ghost. No, she wasn't okay!

"What are you doing out here?" Tina pressed.

Tears flooded Whisper's eyes. She lifted her face to the starry sky. "What does it matter?"

"It matters because it's late. And you're supposed to be at home. In your room. Where it's safe."

"So?"

"*So* you're getting in the car with me. Now."

Whisper wanted to run again. But her body ached, her cooling sweat was starting to make her itch, and she had a side cramp worse than any she'd had running track.

They drove down Hemlock Lane in silence, save the occasional sniffle from Whisper. She couldn't give Tina the satisfaction of seeing her cry. Or of hearing it—*Sounds are grounds, remember?*

Then another sniffle. This one came from Tina. Whisper side-eyed her when they passed under a street-light. Sure enough, Tina's cheeks were streaked with tears.

"Is everything okay with Dad?" Whisper asked.

Another sniffle. "Yes."

Once in the driveway, Tina wiped her eyes and turned to face Whisper. Her sharp chin-length bob swung and settled. "I was really worried about you."

Whisper scoffed.

"You don't believe me?" Tina asked.

"That you care enough to worry? No, I don't."

Tina sat back and stared out at the darkened house.

"It's not easy, Whisper, joining a family like yours. One that's suffered such loss. It's hard to know what to say, what to do. But I do care for you and Miles. Very much. I know I'm not your mother, and I'm certainly not trying to replace her. But I *can* mother you. If you'll let me."

An aggressive batch of fresh tears rose from the depths of Whisper's chest. She tried blinking them back down. They refused.

"Your dad talks about your mother a lot," Tina said. "I wish I'd known her. We would've been friends, I'm sure of it." She turned to Whisper again. "If I could change the past, your mom would still be alive, I'd be her friend, and your family would be together again. But I can't."

Whisper peered up at the house. Her house. The house that Paisley and Rayne now called home. Did they miss their old bedrooms? Their kitchen? Their father?

Did they cry themselves to sleep? Did they wish they could change the past, too?

Whisper dried her cheeks on the sleeve of her sweatshirt, regretting having ever sided with Tina's husband. *If I'd been married to her, I'd have moved to another state, too,* she'd once told her friends. How could she have been so insensitive? Like Dad, Tina had lost a spouse. Like Whisper and Miles, Paisley and Rayne had lost a parent.

"If you care so much," Whisper sniffled, "why are you always so mean to me?"

Tina exhaled sharply. "Maybe I am hard on you, and I'm sorry. You seem so much more self-assured than my kids. More independent. Always going out with your friends. Running circles around kids *two* years older than you. Never afraid to speak your mind or stand up for the things you believe in. Never afraid to wear beanies in summer."

Whisper allowed herself the teeniest of smiles.

"You're comfortable in your own skin. Paisley isn't there yet. She doesn't have that inner confidence. Not like you, anyway."

"Ha! Please. Paisley is the most confident girl in our grade. Maybe our whole school. Probably the entire Pacific Northwest!"

Tina laughed but didn't smile. "It's an act. When Paisley's father left, she fell apart. We all did. But she alone refused to show any emotion. She wanted to be tough, probably because I was a mess. It's been very lonely for her."

"What about with her friends?" Whisper asked. She couldn't count the number of times she'd broken down in front of the Grim Sleepers, the number of times they'd consoled her. "Can't she talk to them?"

Tina shook her head. "Paisley didn't want to be known as the girl whose father left, so she focused on . . . I don't know. More superficial things." She sighed. "We're working on it."

No one understood that better than Whisper. After she lost her mother, attention poured in from kids, neighbors, teachers, guidance counselors. She went from being a peppy, carefree middle schooler to a lab rat. Everyone started observing her and asking how she was holding up. Instead of turning into an overtexting, vanilla-scented bully like Paisley, Whisper had started to run.

And run and run and run.

Tears rolled down Whisper's face. Not just for herself. For all of them.

"I'll make you a deal." Tina put a hand on her shoulder. "If you promise never to sneak out again, I will promise never to tell your dad about this."

"Really?"

Tina nodded and unbuckled her seat belt. "Now, if I make tea, will you please tell me what you were doing running down the street like Silas Hoke himself was after you?"

Whisper grimaced. "I can't. There's, like, a code of secrecy."

Tina narrowed her eyes.

"But I could make something up," Whisper suggested. "I've gotten pretty good at telling stories."

Tina brightened. "A story sounds pretty good right now."

"Cool," Whisper said as she opened her door. "I think you'll like it. It's about thumbs."

CHAPTER 24

ZUZU

Swaddled in sheets of fog, with my back against the cool granite of Ginny Baker's headstone, I am at peace. The tree-branch scratches of my pen against the pages of my journal play a funeral dirge. For I am burying Silas Hoke tonight just like he was buried exactly one hundred years ago.

That's right. From this day forward, I will let Silas Hoke rest in peace.

I will stop trying to embody him.

Stop writing the way I imagine he would write.

Stop trying to see the world through his eyes.

I will try to see the world through my own eyes instead.

Whisper, Sophie, Frannie, and Gemma inspired me.

They're so comfortable being themselves.

It's time for me to follow their lead.

So, dear journal, this is what's on Zuzu Otsuka's mind tonight.

Death.

Why do people fear it? Death is way more predictable than life.

Look around.

Nothing in Crimson Creek Cemetery ever changes. My dead friends are exactly where I expect them to be.

But life? Life is scary. You never know what's going to happen. There is so much to dread.

Dread.

Dead.

Funny how the letter *R* changes everything.

Some might argue that the difference isn't that big. That *dread* and *dead* are connected since most people dread being dead.

I think they are wrong.

I believe dead feels like nothing. But dread feels like trying to digest a fireball.

Trust me. Later tonight, I'm going to the high school football game with Paisley and Miranda, and I've got five-alarm fireball heartburn.

I'm so over pretending I have crushes on jocks who are, like, five years older than me. Over posing and posting and pinging.

But I must show up.

I bailed on them last night so I could meet up with the Grim Sleepers.

I told them the most effective lie I have: that my mom needed me for a last-minute Jōhin photo shoot. If I bail tonight, too, they'll know something is up. And as much as I like Paisley and Miranda—as much as they truly *are* my friends—they can't know something is up.

The Grim Sleepers want to keep their club private, and I need to respect that.

Oh, who am I kidding? It's mostly because Miranda and Paisley don't take betrayal lightly. Just ask Frannie. Or Kelsey. Or Olivia, Charley, Holly, Alexandra, Tamika, Eden, Charlotte, and Mia.

Not familiar with their names?

Exactly.

CHAPTER 25

WHISPER

With Gemma in the lead, the Grim Sleepers wound their way between headstones of every variety: concrete cherubs with faces distorted by cracks, moss-covered granite blocks like the shoulders of rising monsters, and marble crosses coated with spiderwebs.

Whisper tried to focus on the trinkets jangling inside Gemma's bag, the distant smell of woodsmoke, the past night's breakthrough with Tina. Anything to take her mind off the exploding light bulb on Friday and whatever sent them running for their lives on Tuesday night.

Terrified as she was, Whisper wasn't screaming or whimpering or begging them to turn around. She wasn't digging her fingernails into a friend's arm or faking a sudden bout of food poisoning. Her muddy sneakers were pointed in the same direction as everyone else's. She'd come a long way.

It helped that it was only eight o'clock on Saturday night. And that she'd asked Tina for permission to go out.

And that she could see Zuzu up ahead, leaning against Ginny Baker's gravestone as if it were her school locker. In other words, no more jump scares.

"Hey," Zuzu said. "Rad robes. Did you just get out of the shower?"

"They're cloaks," Gemma corrected.

"I know, I'm kidding." Zuzu's playful smile quickly faded. "At least you look like Grim Sleepers." She indicated her outfit: a plaid skirt, charcoal leggings, a denim blazer, and gray high-tops with fuchsia laces. Piled high atop her head was all her hair except the purple wisps that knifed the edges of her face. "I mean, this hardly screams *cemetery*."

"As long as it screams something," Frannie said, offering her a high-five. "Am I right?"

They slapped palms and giggled.

"I thought we could mark the anniversary by giving it the full Grim Sleepers treatment." Gemma tap-tapped her duffel bag of ritualistic objects. "Sorry, Zuzu," she said, not looking sorry at all. "I should have told you to wear something black. My bad."

If Zuzu felt slighted, she didn't show it. She reached for the Jōhin garment bag slung over Ginny's monument and held it above her head like a winning trophy. "All good. I have a solution."

"Of course you do," Gemma muttered.

"What's in the bag?" Sophie asked.

"A surprise. But first, Gemma, did you pick up anything on the G-Tone last night?"

"I, well—The app had some, uh, technical difficulties. I emailed customer service. As soon as I hear back, I'll—"

"I can give it a try," Zuzu offered. "I'm pretty good at that stuff. How do you think I sent those anonymous texts?"

Gemma kicked her duffel bag in Zuzu's direction. "Here, take it."

"Huh?"

"You want to take over so badly, go for it. I don't even care anymore."

Which was Gemma for *I care too much.*

Zuzu's hand flew to her heart. "I'm not trying to take over. I'm trying to help."

"Then what? Pretend you don't know us every time Paisley and Miranda are around?" Gemma's nostrils flared and her blue eyes narrowed with rage.

Being surrounded by dead people was scary, Whisper thought. But Gemma giving up on the Grim Sleepers? That was utterly terrifying. She was the wicked heart and dark soul of the Grim Sleepers. They couldn't do it without her.

"You're right." Zuzu draped the garment bag back over the tombstone. "But not about me wanting to take over. It's your club. I just want to be part of it. What you're right about is the whole Paisley-Miranda thing. I need to be honest with them *because* they're my friends. I know you girls don't like them. They're definitely not perfect. But that doesn't mean I haven't gone through stuff with them. That I don't care for them." Zuzu looked around at the girls. "You all care for each other, right? And I'm sure you've all made mistakes."

The girls shuffled their feet. Whisper, too, until clouds of grave dust began to rise. Better not to irritate the dead with too much shuffling. Especially when the dead—in this case, Ginny Baker—had a whole missing leg to be irritated about.

"Miranda hasn't, like, said anything, has she?" Frannie sounded worried.

"About what? You getting the lead in the musical? 'Cuz, yeah, she has a lot to say about that."

"No," Frannie said. "About you hanging out with us."

Zuzu shook her head. "I would never tell them about the club if that's what you're worried about. But I shouldn't hide that we're friends. I'll work on that. I promise." She paused. "We *are* friends, right?"

The girls looked at Gemma. Gemma tightened her robe.

Whisper nervously blurted, "Did I mention Tina and I are cool now?" It was a rhetorical question: she had mentioned it three times. Her point? *If Tina and I can do it, Zuzu, so can you!*

Frannie bit her nail.

Sophie peeked at her phone.

Zuzu blew a cinnamon-scented bubble.

Pop!

"Will you help me with the G-Tone app?" Gemma finally asked.

"Of course," Zuzu said.

Whisper's shoulders relaxed away from her ears. "And will you stop scaring us? Unless it's your turn to tell a story? And even then, I'm begging you, no props."

"Promise."

"Will you show us what's in the bag?" Sophie asked.

"I will."

Gemma sighed, long and hard. "Will you help us take this club to the next level?"

"Are you sure you're ready?" Zuzu asked with a provocative half smile. No wonder she was Jōhin's muse. She had that magical *thing*. Invisible and impossible to describe, it cast a spell on everyone who saw her. Made them want to wear what she wore, do what she did, be where she was. In this case: a creepy cemetery.

"We're in middle school now." Gemma smirked, giving in to the magic. "So yeah, if you have any ideas, I think we're ready for an upgrade."

"That's what I like to hear." Zuzu opened her journal to a fresh page and click-clicked her pen. "Maybe instead of sleepovers, we gather somewhere, you know, *scary*."

Whisper felt a prickle of concern. Bedrooms were safe. "Where else can we go?"

"If you say the prison, this friendship is over," Frannie said.

"Not the prison." Zuzu stretched her arms wide. "Right here."

Gemma gazed around and exhaled. "It's definitely a step up."

"It's more than a step," Whisper said. "It's an entire staircase."

The others looked so hopeful, though. Excited, even.

"Fine, I'm in," Whisper said. After all, she'd surprised herself with "1-2-3-4, I Declare a Thumb War." Clearly she was capable of more than she'd thought. "There's just one thing. We can't be the Grim Sleepers if we're not doing sleepovers."

"Whisper's right," Gemma said. "We need a new name."

"Yes!" Sophie said. "I love a brainstorm. What about the Sick Clique?"

"The Sin Sisters!" Zuzu suggested.

After that, the ideas came so furiously, Whisper couldn't be sure who shouted what.

"Bad Scare Day!"

"Little Bo Creeps!"

"The She-mons!"

"Ghouls' Night Out!"

"Silent but Deadly!"

"The Ghostests with the Mostest!"

"The Exor-sisters!"

"The Legends of Creepy Hollow!"

"SpongeBob ScarePants!"

"The Hoke's on You!"

"The Fearless Five!"

While the brainstorming continued and their laughter swelled, Whisper peered out at the old cemetery—the eerie shadows, cracked tombstones, and neglected grounds—and tried to imagine meeting here next month, the month after that, the month after that. Was she, Whisper Martin, longtime fraidy-cat, brave enough to become a graveyard girl?

Graveyard Girls.

There was a flutter inside her chest. A shot of tingly heat at the base of her neck. It was as if those two words were trapped inside Whisper's body and begging her to release them into the world where they belonged.

"What about Graveyard Girls?"

Frannie looked at Sophie. Sophie looked at Zuzu. Zuzu looked at Gemma. Gemma looked at Whisper.

Done. No one had to say a word.

Whisper beamed. Her second triumph at Crimson Creek Cemetery. Who could have imagined it?

Gemma held up her duffel bag. "This stuff probably needs an upgrade, too."

"I know!" Zuzu said. "They can be anniversary presents for Silas."

Frannie looked skeptical. "Why would we give presents to a murderer?"

"No one says, *When I grow up, I want to be a murderer,*" Zuzu explained. "Something had to go really wrong in his life for him to do what he did." She peeled off a piece of blue nail polish. "Think of every horror movie villain ever. Either they were born twisted or they were bullied or abused until finally they snapped! I hate what Hoke did as much as anyone else. But I also feel bad for him. His life sucked."

Whisper had never thought of it like that before. But she had come to realize there were two sides to every rivalry. Her talk with Tina proved it. Maybe Zuzu was right. Maybe Silas did deserve a bit of kindness. Who knows? If someone had showed him compassion when he was alive, maybe his life would have turned out differently.

Gemma opened her bag. "Everyone take something."

Frannie grabbed the Chalice of Cherubs.

Sophie selected the box where they stowed their phones during storytelling.

Gemma chose the busted sticks of incense.

Whisper picked the script bearing their incantation.

Zuzu didn't pick up anything. Instead, she held out her hand. "Those robes. Hand them over."

Whisper felt a pang of loss. Sure, the robes were faded, scraggly, and embarrassing. But they'd been there from the beginning. Losing them would be like losing themselves.

"Maybe this will convince you," Zuzu said. With a sly smile, she unzipped the garment bag. In a single graceful movement—the kind she displayed in social media videos every day—she removed five shiny black cloaks.

"The satin was left over from last year's Halloween show. I've been hemming them all day."

The girls were speechless as Zuzu handed out the new cloaks. The fabric was so slippery smooth, Whisper nearly dropped it. "Wait," she said, noticing thin red embroidery on the back. It read: LAURIE STRODE.

"Did this belong to someone else?"

The others squinted at the names on their own cloaks, just as confused.

"I know you want to keep your club secret," Zuzu said. "So I gave us code names. Names that pay homage to horror's greatest final girls."

"What's a final girl?" Sophie asked.

"A final girl is the girl who makes it all the way to the end of the horror movie, even after everyone else gets filleted."

Zuzu held up her own cloak. It read: SIDNEY PRESCOTT.

"From the Scream movies," she explained. "Sidney's kind of like me. She knows everything there is to know about horror."

"Who's Laurie Strode?" Whisper asked.

"Only the hero of five different movies in the Halloween franchise. She reminded me of you, Whisper. Afraid at the beginning but getting stronger along the way."

Whisper liked the sound of that.

Sophie held up her cloak: KIRSTY COTTON.

"Kirsty Cotton is the final girl in several Hellraiser movies," Zuzu said. "Kirsty might be the smartest final girl there is. That's why I thought of you, Sophie."

Sophie ran her fingers over the stitched name, apparently forgetting about her phone for once. "Thank you."

Frannie held up her cloak: TINA SHEPARD.

Zuzu's eyes went big. "There are eleven—count 'em—eleven Friday the 13th movies, plus a remake, plus a TV show. And out of all those final girls, Tina Shepard is the best, the only one who fought off Jason Voorhees with telekinetic powers. That's why I gave her name to you, Frannie. She's a showstopper, too."

"It is easier to say than Francine Vargas-Stein," Frannie admitted.

Gemma held up hers: NANCY THOMPSON.

Zuzu grinned like this was her favorite of all. "Ah, Nancy. The star of three films in the Nightmare on Elm Street series. Nancy starts off a scared kid, but she quickly becomes a leader. In *A Nightmare on Elm Street 3*, she teaches survival techniques to all the dream warriors."

Gemma couldn't hide her grin. "Okay, that sounds pretty dope."

Once Gemma began putting on her new cloak, they all did. The black silk winked in the night like Crimson

Creek through the trees. Whisper pulled the hood over her head. She didn't know much about Laurie Strode—yet—but she felt Laurie's power dart through her veins. The look on her friends' faces said they all felt the same.

Zuzu gestured in the direction of Silas Hoke's grave, giving Gemma room to go first, as usual.

Gemma refused. "You know this place better than anyone, Sidney. Lead the way."

Zuzu winked back. "Sure thing, Nancy."

Onward they crept, through thick fog, past collapsed stones and shattered statues. If not for their glossy new cloaks, Whisper didn't know if they'd be able to see one another. Aside from Sophie, of course. Her phone was back and shining like a lighthouse beacon. When had she become so obsessed?

Whisper edged closer to Sophie. For safety, not snooping, but she saw the screen anyway.

Someone named DANGER ME had texted her:

So I hear you like to sneak out at night.

Sophie was taut with excitement. She'd positioned her fingers upon the keypad, ready to reply, when Frannie accidentally collided with her.

"You almost made me drop my . . ." Sophie's angry expression softened; her pinched features expanded as she looked down.

"Soph?" Frannie prodded.

No reply.

Whisper waved a hand in front of her friend's frozen face. "Sophie!"

A yawn of wind shifted the fog, revealing Zuzu and Gemma. Each was clutching her anniversary gifts so hard, her fingers had gone pale. Their eyes were cast downward, their faces rigid with fear.

A few seconds ago, Whisper had felt like a heroic final girl eager to broaden her bravery, forge new rituals, and tell horrifying new stories. She'd even felt ready to forgive murderers.

But this final girl's story couldn't continue until she looked down.

As the ghostly veil of fog ribboned away, she did.

Silas Hokes's headstone was right in front of them, right where it had always been.

But the grave had been dug up. It was open and empty.

No coffin.

Just a wormy, earthy hole.

The Graveyard Girls had arrived.

But Silas Hoke was gone.

ACKNOWLEDGMENTS

Come, ghost,
Come, monster,
Come, devilkin,
So many people to thank,
So let us begin. . . .

Chief creative officer and publisher at Union Square & Co., Emily Meehan, heard our pitch for Graveyard Girls and gave it a big thumbs-up. (Yes, pun intended. Duh.) Emily, thank you so much for believing in us and this concept. Thank you to our editor, Tracey Keevan, for taking said concept and blowing our minds with your enthusiasm and creative vision. Samantha Knoerzer, thank you for not blocking us and/or quitting when we inundated your inbox with Word documents during our frenzied writing process. We have a streamlined system now. You're welcome.

Okay, so, you know the stunning cover of Graveyard Girls? The one you wish you could wallpaper your bedroom with? And you know the design and illustrations on the interior pages? We did all of that.

Kidding.

Illustrator Flavia Sorrentino, creative director Melissa Farris, creative director Jo Obarowski, art director Whitney Manger, and designer Christine Heun get credit for that. (But the wallpaper was our idea.) As long as we're being honest, we can't take credit for the novel's impeccable spelling and grammar, either. Kayla Overbey and Margaret Moore paid attention in school while we were daydreaming and now they're brilliant copy editors who save daydreamers on the regular. Thank you for being good students.

Thank you, Renee Yewdaev and Kevin Iwano, for getting this book out the door and into your hands (or ears).

Thank you, Richard Abate, our feared and fearless agent, and Martha Stevens for keeping us all afloat. Finally, thank you to the voices in our heads. Keep talking. We need you.

Lisi & Daniel

ABOUT THE AUTHORS

Suzanne Plunkett

DANIEL KRAUS is a *New York Times* best-selling author. His posthumous collaboration with legendary filmmaker George A. Romero, *The Living Dead*, was acclaimed by *The New York Times* and *The Washington Post*. Kraus's *The Death and Life of Zebulon Finch* was named one of *Entertainment Weekly*'s Top 10 Books of the Year. With Guillermo del Toro, he co-authored *The Shape of Water*, based on the same idea the two created for the Oscar-winning film. Also with del Toro, Kraus co-authored *Trollhunters*, which was adapted into the Emmy-winning Netflix series. Kraus has won a Scribe Award, two Odyssey Awards (for both *Rotters* and *Scowler*) and has been a Library Guild selection, YALSA Best Fiction for Young Adults, multiple Bram Stoker finalist, and more. Kraus's work has been translated into over twenty-five languages. Visit him at danielkraus.com.

LISI HARRISON worked at MTV Networks in New York City for twelve years. She left her position as senior director of development in 2003 to write The Clique series, which sold more than eight million copies and was on *The New York Times* best seller list for more than two hundred weeks. Ten of the titles hit #1 and foreign rights sold in thirty-three countries. The Alphas was a #1 *New York Times* best seller, and *Monster High* was an instant best seller. In 2013 she released her YA series Pretenders and her first adult novel, *The Dirty Book Club* in 2017. In 2021 Lisi launched two new middle-grade series—Girl Stuff in February and The Pack in June. Lisi lives in Laguna Beach, California, where she runs workshops that teach girls how to have drama-free friendships. For more information on Lisi's novels and workshops visit LisiHarrison.com.

Graveyard Girls book two sneak peek!

SCREAM
FOR THE CAMERA

CHAPTER 1

SOPHIE

"Idea!" Sophie said, with the spontaneity of someone who hadn't been scheming for the better half of Wednesday morning. "Let's eat lunch outside!" She ditched her orange tray in favor of a to-go salad. "This cafeteria smells like a dead pig's butt."

"Dead," Whisper said, flatly.

"*Un*-dead," Gemma muttered.

"So you're actually going there," Frannie said.

It was impossible not to. They couldn't hear the word *dead* without thinking *un*. And they couldn't think *un* without thinking of last month's discovery: Silas Hoke's dug-up grave and his missing corpse. The missing corpse that had yet to be *un*-missing.

"Yeah, fresh air would be good," Whisper said.

Frannie nodded in agreement. So did her brown curls.

As always, Gemma led the way.

Upon leaving the cafeteria, Sophie glimpsed Zuzu Otsuka.

Last month, Zuzu had begged Sophie, Gemma, Whisper, and Frannie to let her join the Graveyard Girls, their very exclusive, top secret scary-story club. But Zuzu had yet to tell Paisley and Miranda she had made new friends. Because the club was top secret? Hardly. Zuzu's omission was far less honorable. Irony alert: the horror-obsessed "it girl" was afraid.

Why? Well, Sophie had four theories:

1. Paisley and Miranda weren't into "new friends." New friends took attention off *them* and attention was their cardio.

2. They wouldn't approve of Sophie (academic overachiever), Whisper (loud-voiced, beanie-wearing, track-star environmentalist), Frannie (future superstar of stage and screen), and Gemma (incense-scented believer in all things otherworldly). Because, according to Paisley and Miranda, girls like them weren't "post-worthy." And if you're not post-worthy you're not . . . well, you're just not.

3. Getting on the bad sides of Paisley and Miranda was like hurling yourself into an active volcano. It burned.

4. All of the above.

Outside, the girls settled on the brick embankment near the bicycle racks and set out their lunches.

"It's been four weeks since Silas Hoke's body went missing from his grave," Gemma said. Sophie knew Gemma couldn't help herself. Gemma was obsessed. They all were.

Whisper pulled her green beanie a little lower. "No corpse talk while we're eating."

"Gemma's right, though," Frannie said. "Four weeks—and not a single person has noticed? It's not on the news. Not in the local papers. It's like it never happened. I smell a cover-up."

Whisper fanned the air. "I smell your onion rings."

"Something's not right," Gemma said.

"Frannie's breath," Whisper said.

"What if we imagined it?" Gemma asked, determined to stay on track.

"Frannie's breath?" Whisper asked.

While the others laughed, Sophie crunched a celery stick and tried to recall the night they stumbled on the open grave. It had only been a month, and yet so many details had gone fuzzy. And she knew why.

Lately, Sophie had been distracted. And by *distracted* she meant *obsessed* with the boy she'd code-named "Danger Me"—which is what Dane Jeremy's name sounded like if you said it fast, which Sophie did, over and over, to herself.

Was that pathetic? Absolutely, but Sophie's crush had possessed her like a malevolent spirit in one of Zuzu's horror films. For the first time in her life, she felt out of control. And it was kind of glorious.

Sophie met Danger Me at the Julian Academy of Music a few months back—if "met" was the right word to describe making faces at each other through the soundproof window dividing Sophie's piano studio from Danger Me's guitar lessons. After Danger Me Airdropped his number, the two had started texting.

A lot.

Like, a *lot* lot.

Enough that her older sister, Jade, had warned her it was too much, too fast.

But Miss Overachieving-Perfect-At-Everything Jade didn't know everything. Just most things. The true nature of Sophie's text relationship with Danger Me was not one of them.

No one knew how intense it had become. Not even her best friends. There was also another secret. Because of this delicious distraction, Sophie's A+ average was starting to resemble Antonín Dvořák's cello concerto—a solid score of B minor.

Was she proud of these secrets? Obviously not. At the same time, Sophie wasn't making any effort to improve. After years of intense studying, endless pressure, and overscheduling, these text exchanges with Danger Me felt like vacation. A flirtation vacation. A *flircation*.

Sophie's phone chimed.

Yes!

This was why she *really* wanted to eat outside. Principal Vazquez had recently instituted a no-phones-in-the-cafeteria-unless-you-want-them-confiscated rule. No way was Sophie going to risk that. Her phone was the only way she could communicate with Danger Me. And *not* communicating with Danger Me was *not* an option. So she casually angled her body away from the girls and returned to her flircation location—a distant island known for its belly butterflies and coconut-scented secrets. A place she wanted to stay forever.